YA ZEITOUN
Zeitoun, Mary-Lou,
Jamilah at the end of the world /

JAMILAH AT THE END OF THE WORLD

MARY-LOU ZEITOUN

James Lorimer & Company Ltd., Publishers
Toronto

James Lorimer & Company Ltd., Publishers acknowledges funding support from the Ontario Arts Council (OAC), an agency of the Government of Ontario. We acknowledge the support of the Canada Council for the Arts, which last year invested $153 million to bring the arts to Canadians throughout the country. This project has been made possible in part by the Government of Canada and with the support of Ontario Creates.

Cover design: Rosie Gowsell
Cover image: Shutterstock

Library and Archives Canada Cataloguing in Publication (Paperback)

Title: Jamilah at the end of the world / Mary-Lou Zeitoun.
Names: Zeitoun, Mary-Lou, author.
Identifiers: Canadiana (print) 20210207825 | Canadiana (ebook) 20210207841 | ISBN 9781459416482 (softcover) | ISBN 9781459416499 (EPUB)
Classification: LCC PS8599.E37 J36 2021 | DDC C813/.6—dc2

Published by:
James Lorimer & Company
Ltd., Publishers
117 Peter Street, Suite 304
Toronto, ON, Canada
M5V 0M3
www.lorimer.ca

Distributed in Canada by:
Formac Lorimer Books
5502 Atlantic Street
Halifax, NS, Canada
B3H 1G4
www.formac.ca

Distributed in the US by:
Lerner Publisher Services
241 1st Ave. N.
Minneapolis, MN, USA
55401
www.lernerbooks.com

Printed and bound in Canada.
Manufactured by Friesens Corporation in Altona, Manitoba, Canada in June 2021.
Job #277235

For my Teta Jamileh Zeitoun.

Survival Tip #1

How to Build a Shelter

If you are outside, find a place that is dry, flat, not next to a body of water and has a good place for a fire. Tie a tarp between two trees, or tie a cord between two trees and drape a tarp over it. Weigh it down with rocks on either side. Or grab a bunch of tall sticks and make a teepee.

> (I tried in the backyard — mine didn't work. The sticks kept falling over everything.)

A long-term solution for safety is a bunker. A bunker is a defensive military fortification designed to protect people and valued materials from falling bombs or other attacks. Bunkers are mostly underground, in contrast to blockhouses, which are mostly above ground.

> (Every kid loves forts. But maybe I liked them a little too much. I draped blankets and sheets over the couch and end tables in the living room. I liked how the fort walls almost touched me and how the light inside became the colour of the fabric walls. Unfortunately, my mom and dad did not appreciate how I emptied the linen closet. And I am a klutz, so a lot of innocent lamps died in the process.)

CHAPTER 1
There Is No Planet B

My name is Jamilah Mansour and I need to do something, because CLIMATE CHANGE. I'm seventeen. My dad is a Palestinian immigrant from, like, thirty years ago and my mom is old-timey Anglo Canadian. He's a pharmacist and Mom's a naturopath. We live in Toronto, Canada. So that's like a normal background here, really. It's me, Mom and Dad, my fifteen-year-old sister Noor, my twelve-year-old brother George and Teta (pronounced "Tayta") in the granny suite downstairs.

To be honest, my bunker obsession had been going on for a while. I think it started when I was little and saw a Totally Awful American Hurricane on TV — the desperate people stuck in gridlocks on highways and trapped in sports stadiums. The worst thing in the TV coverage was the families waiting to be rescued on roofs. There was a dog they had to leave behind because it couldn't fit into the helicopter rescue basket. When the camera pulled back you could see the animals left behind, the cats were miserable and terrified smudges in the corners because cats hate open spaces and loud noises. That's what got me. I think I have PTSD from seeing the people on the roofs and the pets dying.

So I just needed to build a safe place, to prepare and protect my family in case of a climate disaster. Sure, people like my sister, Noor, go to protests and marches all the time. But what's the point of marches? People have been marching since the eighties and the climate's, like, worse now. In fact, I don't even see the point of going to university. I'd rather spend my time doing something useful. By the time I got my basic, general BA (because my math scores were so bad, even though I love science, I couldn't go into science), the world would have imploded into anarchic city states run by militia. Because — hello — *climate change*. I figured I could use the time to convert the garage into an off-the-grid tiny house. A bunker, really. In case you didn't know, a bunker is a doom room, a safe space, a place where you store food, water and even weapons. I was also going to find a way to get a generator.

We were in a terrible heat wave when I first inspected the garage for bunker possibilities. I went out back and pulled on its side door. It stuck at first, then popped open. A waft of mildewy air hit my face as I looked around. I saw an elliptical machine and a recumbent exercise bike, which were moved out of the basement when Teta got here. Leaning against a full-length cracked mirror was a half-rolled carpet. In the middle was a big, green painted dresser with a black garbage bag squatting on top of it, half open and spilling baby clothes. I opened a dresser drawer. It was empty except for a scattering of mice poop. The space was about ten by fourteen feet. The cinder-block element was good. You could do a lot with cinder blocks. They're good for insulation, are fireproof and are easy to paint.

Yes, this would make an excellent bunker. I slowly turned. One wall was lined with rickety shelves full of plastic bins. Our leaking fibreglass canoe hung from the ceiling (I'd have to save that in case of a flood). Past the jumble of busted bikes by the door was an entire shelf filled with broken coffee makers, lamps and even ashtrays from when Mom used to smoke. I could work with this. No one was using the garage anyway. Mom and Dad never parked the car in it because the alley leading up to it was too narrow. So the garage was always used as, let's face it, a dumping ground. Mom had painted the wall that faced the backyard bright blue with a fake window, complete with a flower box, which looked totally pathetic and not cheerful.

I approached Mom and Dad at breakfast. CBC Radio was muttering in the background as always. Mom was having her protein shake with organic blueberries, organic whey protein and flaxseed oil. She was all about clean eating and crystals. And she bleached her hair. I'm just saying. Even though she was a vegetarian naturopath she put purple streaks in her hair that, I liked to remind her, required a highly toxic bleaching process first.

Dad was eating za'atar, dipping pieces of pita into the dried herbal mixture of thyme, sumac and sesame seeds. He was very picky about his za'atar, buying only Palestinian brands and even scoffing at the Lebanese and Syrian formulas. Dad's a pretty mild guy. But if you want to make him mad, show him an Israeli fusion restaurant menu that lists za'atar, or any Palestinian food, as Israeli cuisine. Whew! He'll, like, yell at the manager.

Otherwise, we are not very political. We are Christian Arabs, which is really annoying because nobody thinks that's a thing (it's Jesus of *Nazareth*, not *Dublin* — jeez). Uncle Gabrielle always says, "The angry mob isn't going to stop to ask this difference," when we come up against Islamophobia. Aunt Lily, who writes a lifestyle blog for the *Globe and Mail*, agrees. She gets a lot of snooty readers who are surprised she is so sophisticated *and* Palestinian. The most we ever do Palestinian-wise is go to folk dances at the Arab Centre, eat Arabic food and, lately, translate for and volunteer with the Syrian refugees. Okay, we go to the Toronto Palestinian Film Festival every fall, too. It's true, sometimes my grandmother, who lives downstairs, cries because she remembers things from the old country.

Anyway, I am not political that way. My best friend, Vivian, and I never talk about it, and she's Jewish. I mean, she has birthright and goes to Israel every year. So when she goes for vacation, we always give her things to give to my great aunts in Haifa.

I sauntered over to Dad and tore a piece of bread to dip into the olive oil and then the za'atar. "Can I clean out the garage?" I asked, chewing.

"I would love for you to clean out the garage," said Mom. "I would even pay you for the job!"

"Thank you!" I headed back to the garage. "It will make an excellent bunker."

"No, then we'll use it to park the car!" she called after me.

I came back. "Mom, we need to have a safe space off the grid in case of a natural disaster or power outage. Don't you understand?" I asked.

"Why do you worry about these things?" asked Dad. "Put your energy into university."

I hadn't told them I wasn't going yet.

"Did you have your calm tea today?" asked Mom. "I made a batch for you. It's in the fridge."

"You know what would make me calm?" I asked. "Knowing we had a safe house when the power grid goes down."

"This is not the end of the world," said Dad. "In Gaza they just take the power away all the time. It comes back."

"You know what?" I said. "What if it doesn't come back? Like, because there isn't any? 'Cause your generation used it all up!"

"It's that Desmond with his conspiracy theories that's making you like this!" said Mom.

Oh, here we go. Desmond is my childhood buddy and he's a touchy subject. Mom thought he needed a diagnosis. He is smart and funny, but he had smoked so much pot since like, age eleven, that all he did was hang in his parents' basement, play video games and sext stupid basics.

I didn't even know how they could type, these girls were so basic. "I'm so hot for you," they typed, probably crippled as much by their fake nails as their feeble brains. They probably got more confused figuring out the logistics of their reflection selfies than a cat looking in the mirror for the first time.

It's true that Desmond followed conspiracy theories. I mean, he was still on the 9/11 conspiracy. He is mixed Black, so I kept telling him that he didn't even *need* a theory to be paranoid, that the culture is actually, openly against him. It's right out there. He and I used to go to the games store and skateboard and roam the city on the subway together. But when he started smoking more, we just ended up hanging out on his couch and watching Lord of the Rings-type movies. He was very into those old-timey medieval sagas. Put an actor in armour and give him an English accent and Desmond was down.

Maybe I didn't like the Insta girls because I couldn't be like that. Insta was thirsty and embarrassing, yes, but I honestly didn't have the confidence to post. I'm a thicker girl. Even though that's almost cool now, skinny girls still rule. They are like another species to me. My interactions with boys had been limited to a little kissing at parties and having crushes on actors. In the interest of having a life the year before, I hooked up with Marley a few times at his house. Marley had brown sweeping eyebrows and a square jaw and those carved square thumbs boys have (there's a reason why I was with him). But I felt like Marley forgot I was there when he was touching me. Apparently, you are supposed to be so attracted you don't care about that stuff.

Desmond was tall with broad shoulders and he would have been cute if he didn't always look like he'd been hit by a tranquilizer gun.

9

And if he didn't smell funky. Honestly, he was barely human anymore, let alone male. I also think the chicks he was texting were getting skankier and skankier because he had no sex drive left. Vivian, who is in her second year of psychology at university (she's incredibly smart and went early), says if you become an incredibly creative masturbator or get too into porn, then you can't have regular sex anymore. Desmond was not going to university either. He actually hadn't gone to school last year for even one day. *One day.* His parents didn't even realize it.

"No, Mom," I said to my mom's suggestion. "It's not Desmond. Even Toronto Hydro says so! Look!" I ran to the jumble of mail on the kitchen counter and grabbed the hydro bill.

I had started reading and rereading the brochures that came with the hydro bills, searching for clues that they were warning us the power grid was going to fail. Even the way the hydro bill was designed was getting alarming.

"Summer storm a-brewing? Don't be caught off guard. Update your 72-hour emergency kit so you're set all summer. Add in extra bottled water, rain gear and sunscreen. Don't forget to check batteries and to make sure the kit is waterproof."

Mom looked at the scary, cheerful brochure. The winter one had said, "Be Prepared" next to stick figures of a mom, a dad and a kid. Under the stick figures was a snow cloud with lightning coming out of it. The stick family had blank circle faces and didn't seem at all upset about the weather. "Winter is Coming" said the brochure (like hydro had never heard of that cosplay fantasy show or, like, worse, there was some dank nerd in the copy department who got away with it). Then it listed ways to protect yourself. *Most* scary: fill your vehicle with gas.

"We don't even have a seventy-two-hour emergency kit!" I looked at my dad. He was totally chill and still eating his za'atar.

"Dad, I think we at least need to store water," I said. "Can we buy more water bottles? The big kind?"

"This is expensive. We will fill what we have with the tap water." Dad was of the opinion that Toronto tap water was the best in the world. Whenever we came home from Montreal or the US to visit our cousins, he'd get a glass of water from the sink and go, "Ahhh, delicious Toronto tap water."

"Okay, but the tap water is filled with estrogen and mercury," I said.

He shrugged.

Dad didn't argue the need for hoarding water, because hoarding water was normal in the old country. He just didn't want to waste money. We were so in debt for our shabby west-end Victorian brownstone it wasn't funny. Our house was basically rotting. It had a great front porch, but the floorboards creaked and sagged, and the railing was wobbly. Our roof was dotted with little cages, supposed to prevent and capture any squirrels trying to sneak in. The bricks were crumbling and the backyard lawn was mostly weeds, with a BBQ and plastic chairs on concrete pavers. Noor had made a few little fairy gardens in some corners and under bushes, which was kinda cute.

Noor is a genius and super condescending. She hates that I am so emotional and messy, and is always calling me needy. (Noor ironically means "light" and yes, she does think she is Queen Noor of Jordan.) Noor gets away with everything, including being queer, which my mom loves and Dad ignores. I, as the oldest girl, got away with *nothing* while Dad was trying to figure out what was cool for girls in Canada. Of course, then George the total prince comes along and he gets whatever he wants. Downside for George — they are already grooming him to be a doctor. I keep failing math, so they expect me to be, like, a teacher.

The only thing Noor and I agree on is global warming, but we have different approaches. She's all activist and makes signs and does school strikes and marches. She marches for everything: BLM, LGBTQ rights, Indigenous sovereignty. She is Miss Intersectional. I had gone to a few school strikes and marches with her, but got terrible anxiety when I was suddenly crushed by people and couldn't move in front of Queen's Park. At one point I had to pee really bad, so I tried to squeeze through one of those metal guardrails. It toppled over and I fell with it, scraping my knee. A cop helped me up and led me out of the crowd. I just took the subway home alone with that bleeding knee, clutching my sign that said "There is No Planet B" upside down. So yeah, I am not into protests.

Survival Tip #2

How to Harvest Fresh Water from a Plant

Tie a plastic bag around some leaves of a tree or bush and put something heavy, like a rock, in the bag to weigh it down to create a reservoir. After twenty-four hours or so, you should have at least a cup of water.

(I did this with a piece of the grapevine in the backyard, but the next day there was no water and hell to pay when Dad came out and saw the branch, bent from the weight of the rock and wrapped in a plastic bag like a hostage. He nursed it back, though.)

CHAPTER 2
Winter Is Coming

During the heat wave, I spent hours in the living room with a fan on me, watching the weather network and listening to its plinky horror-movie soundtrack. It's twenty-seven degrees? Livable. When is it forty? How many days of the heat wave? What's the long-term trend? How big are the fires in British Columbia? I started to check and recheck the weather app on my phone. It showed daily highs and overnight lows and the air pollution index. They became the boundaries of my life — special weather alerts and thirty-six-hour trends and fourteen-day trends. What was I looking for?

When the weather app on my phone changed its interface, I was irritable for days. Sometimes there was an angry triangle with an exclamation mark on my phone about a special weather alert, like wind or rainfall. I was worried because, if a heat wave goes on too long, the power grid will go down. If the power grid goes down, the world will go crazy. It's called Anarchy.

George kept interrupting my weather watching to play video games. We have just the one TV, so we all have to deal with him spending hours on the couch killing things and slamming back juice (and energy drinks when Mom isn't looking) in front of everyone.

"Weirdo," he said. "Who watches the weather network?"

"Climate change, dummy," I said. "A lot scarier than your stupid superhero movies."

"Climate change is a hoax," he said, twitching away at the controller.

"Anyway," I said, "you are the weird one. I believe you have worn that hoodie for three months straight."

George scowled at me. Unlike me, who was able to pass with my green eyes and straight brown hair, George was darker skinned with really black, gorgeous curls that he wore like an afro. Also unlike me, he was totally into being white and conservative. Hahaha! Joke's on him! He's the one who looked the most Arabic in the family. I leaned over and grabbed the controller.

"Mom!" screamed George. "Tell Jamilah to let me play my game!"

"Kids, stop fighting," called Mom from the kitchen.

George kicked me sideways and I dropped the controller.

"Are you kidding me?" I said. "Mom, George just kicked me!" Sadly, it was not hard for me to revert to being an eight-year-old. Noor was born forty and I am a perpetual child.

Mom came to the living room. "I want you both to take a break and go to your rooms and do your five-minute meditations," she said.

She had given us all a one-sheet on mindfulness meditation and taught us how to do it. "It's especially good for you, Jamilah, with your anxiety," she had said at the time. "You need to learn the tools now."

During the lesson, Noor basically levitated immediately. George tried not to giggle. I kept saying "It's not working" every five seconds. She still made us do it with her every day for a week. Dad sat in with his amber worry beads and clicked them.

Mom walked over to the coffee table, picked up the remote and turned off the TV.

"Both of you, now! Off you go!" she demanded, pointing upstairs. "I don't want to hear anything but mindfulness for the next five minutes!"

I mean, I know she's a naturopath and all. But somehow, I think real meditation teachers take a different approach with their students.

Survival Tip #3

How to Prepare a Go Bag

A go bag is a bag of necessities you can grab in case of emergency.

(Well, I got this. Everyone makes fun of me because I drag my huge backpack everywhere. And you're supposed to just leave a go bag by the door.)

What to Put in a Go Bag:
- **Three-day supply of water and non-perishable food.**

(Muffins are perishable. Hard way.)

- **Phone charger, battery bank or inverter, battery-powered or hand-crank radio, battery-powered or hand-crank flashlight, extra batteries.**
- **Cash in small bills, emergency blanket, whistle, N95 masks.**

You need a go bag for every member of the household.

(I tried to pack one for George and Noor but they wouldn't give me their old backpacks to use. So I put a water bottle and some crackers in a plastic bag by the doors of their rooms. Mom threw them out and told me to stop leaving junk around.)

CHAPTER 3
Generator Generation

I didn't mind being sent up to my room. I was feeling the need to check out my supply closet. Plus, I had the AC window unit in there, which, I know, is bad for the environment. But I'm no good to anybody if I die of heatstroke before I can set up the bunker. My room was the only one with an AC unit, and my parents had fought even against that because of the hydro bill. But no way I'm sitting in fermenting dead skin and sweat all day. I hate the heat. It makes my skin turn into sticky rubber and my thighs chafe when I walk. I have to wear bicycle shorts under everything.

Until I could convince my parents to really get behind turning the garage into a bunker, I figured I could at least turn my small bedroom closet into an emergency supply cupboard. But it wasn't going so well. I had emptied the closet and shoved all my clothes under the bed and on top of the dresser. Whenever I had anxiety, I opened the closet door and stood in front of it, secretly vaping, my head going dizzy and focused with each nicotine-laced, metallic apple-blossom inhale.

I had started vaping when Desmond gave me a few hits of his. If my mom knew she would kill me. (Teta wouldn't care. She had a hookah in her room that she had crocheted a cover for . . . even the hose!) But now, the only thing that settled my washes of panic was vaping. I was having trouble buying cartridges, though, as they were expensive and I didn't have a job. Not having a job was a problem. Since I wasn't working, Mom made me do the endless washing, drying and folding of all the little white towels that she used for work, a job I had loved for about a month when I was ten and now hated. Up and down the stairs, change the laundry, plus empty the dishwasher over and over again every day. George, of course, never had to do the laundry.

"Everyone else in this household is working or studying," Mom kept saying when I complained.

Noor had a job. She was somehow making, like, hundreds of dollars a day bussing at the hipster coffee shop around the corner. All she did was sneer at the raggedy, old bearded guys in love with her and gently smile at the skinny white moms and their awful babies. She gets, like, a dollar, every time someone even *looks* at her. There are hundreds of loonies just stacked in a corner of her room.

"This is underpaid domestic servitude!" I yelled. I wished I was living in a tree, naked, eating with my hands, like that butterfly girl in the redwoods I read about in one of Mom's naturopath magazines. No dishes. No laundry. Poop off a tree limb into the creek.

Meanwhile, my job was to protect the family from disaster. This is what I had so far in my closet:

- one can of tuna
- two AA batteries (wasn't sure if they worked; needed 400 more)
- no LÄRABARs because I ate them all watching sitcom reruns on my phone
- three big flashlights but they needed D batteries
- two tealights. Damn Noor kept stealing them for her Wiccan stuff
- one gallon of bottled water

- a little, tiny propane burner
- one pack of matches

Oh, man, this was weak. I needed a generator, not a propane burner. The generator I was looking at was portable, low-noise and about $1,999 at Canadian Tire. Low-noise is good. A lot of our neighbours who worked in construction had generators that they ran in winter power outages. They were loud. I wondered if there were solar generators? Obviously, this was going to have to be my parents' contribution. At this rate, we weren't going to last three hours, let alone three days, in a disaster. I needed sunscreen and rain gear and so much more food. Oh, and a cash stash. I had eleven dollars in quarters. Also, well, I'm not an American doomsday prepper, but I guess I was going to have to look into some kind of protection, maybe even guns.

I checked my go bag. It had:
- a dented, unopened plastic water bottle
- two Band-Aids
- a small battery-operated fan
- empty LÄRABAR wrappers
- a lighter
- two tampons
- a compass that used to belong to my grandfather, Sido
- a field guide to edible mushrooms
- a travel-size sunscreen
- hand sanitizer
- a sewing kit
- an extra pair of socks

I was searching for more solar generators when Vivian FaceTimed me from work, which was a restaurant right downtown by the stadium. She was setting up for the lunch rush and taking a smoke break. She smoked real smokes. I looked at her beautiful, straight, honey-coloured hair and her perfect eyelash extensions. Vivian was super smart and her big goal was to be a social media influencer so she could study the psychology of screen interaction. It didn't hurt that she was also getting free stuff because she was almost up to 100,000 followers. But she didn't do the "look how hot I am" posts. She posted about her mini cactus garden or genocides or funny street signs. I could almost get behind social media with her.

She laughed at my vape, expertly pulling a cigarette from her pack while holding her phone, which she never let go of.

"OMG, vaping. You're such a dork. I love it!" she said. She swivelled and held up her phone. "Here with BFF Jamilah . . . nicotine break." She flicked her eyes from the camera to me. "You mind if I put that on Insta?"

"No, don't do that," I said, panicked at the thought of my parents learning I vaped. "We're not supposed to promote vaping, let alone smoking!"

"We gotta quit," sighed Vivian.

"Tomorrow," I said. "Tomorrow we will quit."

"What are you doing?"

"Organizing the emergency cupboard."

"You are too much, Jamimi," she said. "You got to get a grip. Wait, look at this."

She texted me a link, I opened it.

"Ellen Benoit to speak at Global March on Parliament Hill," it said. Ellen was one of Noor's favourite climate activists.

"Look, Jamimi," said Vivian. "She's, like, twelve and she's speaking out and organizing at international conferences. She's from Toronto, too!"

I looked at the clip. A young girl with brown hair was standing on a stage. There were a lot of old men behind her.

"When I was kid," she said (some of the old men snickered),

"everyone told us to recycle every piece of string and glass, to rewash freezer bags or there will be a climate disaster. You made us watch movies of polar bears dying and tsunamis and garbage-filled oceans."

She turned and gave a very good evil eye to one of the old men. Aunt Lily would have been impressed.

"Yes, it's good to eliminate single-use plastics. But we *know* it is the major corporations, reliance on fossil fuels and the industrial complex that's destroying our planet. And government policies."

"We should go to the march," said Vivian. "It'll be fun. Desmond can drive. Road trip!"

"You know how I feel about rallies and protests," I said.

"Mimi!" she said, suddenly stern. Mimi was her short form for Jamilah. "Listen to me. The only way to control your eco-anxiety is to *take action!*"

"Stockpiling for the bunker is taking action," I said.

"In a community, Mimi. By joining a community." She smiled her charm smile.

"Think of all the cute guys who will be there!" she said. "And they'll have the same vibe as you. Think of it, a cute eco-dude in his cargo pants and little pocketknife."

I had to laugh. It would be nice to meet a guy like me. I couldn't imagine a guy having the same vibe as me.

Survival Tip #4

How to Survive a Downed Electricity Line

- Do not touch the line or anything touching the line.

- Stay at least ten metres away.

- Call 911 immediately.

- If you are in a car and help isn't coming, jump out of your vehicle and land with both feet. Do not touch the car and the ground at the same time. Keep calm and shuffle away.

    (The electricity lines came down after a windstorm a couple of years ago. Hydro came and fixed it, but I still didn't go out for the rest of the day in case the electricity was somehow stored in the road. Just in case.)

CHAPTER 4
Thanks, David Suzuki

The more I thought about it, the more I realized you would actually have to be a useful person when the world falls apart, like being able to grow stuff or build things or heal people. But who in my family would be useful? Maybe a pharmacist would come in handy when we are down to the barter system and using weeds as our drugs. I had to learn some skills. I was thinking small-machine repair. Or solar-panel installation.

Mom and Dad were outside gardening when I went to the garage to start emptying it. I pulled out a few bikes and boxes, then casually walked over to Dad, who was tying up the tomatoes.

"Dad," I said, "can I ask you something serious?"

Dad took a few seconds with a tie and looked up.

"How about we get a little generator to help convert the garage into a bunker?" I said nervously. "So we can have an off-the-grid space when it all goes down. You can get it for my birthday."

"We can't afford it, dear," said Mom.

"What about my university money?" Okay. Here it goes. Now was the time. "Because I didn't apply," I said. "I just don't feel there's any point in going to university when we need to prepare for a climate disaster."

"What?" thundered Dad. "You are going to university!"

"I am not! University won't matter when the power grid is

down!" I said. "University would take too long, the oceans will have risen higher, currency will be a thing of the past and we'll be living in a barter system again."

"Jamilah, calm down," said Mom.

"You know what happens to girls in a barter system," I said. "Do you want me to become a sex worker?"

"Do not talk like this!" said Dad.

"Michael, calm down," said Mom. She turned to me. "This has gone too far, Jamilah."

"Well, what did you expect? You raised me on environmental catastrophe!" I said. "Thanks, David Suzuki!"

Teta came up her back stairs that led to the garden. She was on her way to the Portuguese seniors' centre and was holding her beige, leather seventies purse. Teta was tall for an Arab woman, like me. Dad brought her and Sido here to Canada twenty years ago from Haifa, Israel. When Sido died she moved from their rental apartment in Toronto to downstairs with us. Our house smelled constantly of cumin (to white people, cumin smells like sweat, which is why white people think cab drivers are dirty) and cinnamon. She had a kitchen down there, and she was just down there cooking almost every day, making us majadara, kibbeh, grape leaves (if I helped her roll them) and baked spaghetti.

Teta also hung out with the tiny Portuguese ladies who, since they all wore the same housedresses and cheap slip-on mules, looked like a little gang. A gang with sworn allegiance to the Catholic Church, an allegiance so fierce Jesus himself would probably tell them to calm down. Teta has mild, sweet brown eyes and the right eye is usually running a bit. She is a sweet woman like they don't make sweet people anymore. She isn't judgmental, except sometimes she put her broad hand on my bare clavicles and arms when I wore sleeveless tanks and said, "Too much skin." Although she has been here for about twenty years, her French is better than her English. She mostly speaks Arabic to my dad.

"*Khalas, khalas,*" said Teta. She and Dad exchanged a few notes on shopping for dinner. We were having green bean stew, apparently.

Teta could say "*Khalas*" ("enough") all she wanted.

"You still need hope to live," said Mom. "Even Suzuki apologized to his daughter for making her anxious."

"When I was nine, you told me the deadline had already passed for the Tokyo Accord to make a difference," I said. "Now I want to do something about it . . ."

"Well, go to the marches, like Noor!" said Mom. "Remember 'Never doubt that a small group of thoughtful, committed citizens can change the world. Indeed, it is the only thing that ever has.'"

"Okay, Boomer," I said. Hollow sayings were unhelpful when we could be out of water and food.

"You can't be filling your head with this end of the world stuff," said Dad. "It's unhealthy. You already have anxiety. Everything will be okay."

"Guess what else is unhealthy?" I shouted. "The world being on fire!"

I stomped into the kitchen and poured water into the saucepan for tea, which is how we made hot beverages because our electric kettle died two years ago and we never replaced it. Noor appeared silently in the kitchen doorway. Her hair was about half an inch long and dyed lavender.

Noor has always been ahead of her time. She identifies as sexually fluid, which is perfect because she hates everyone equally. She was dating Beth, a very butch lesbian who dressed exactly like an English private school boy. Right down to the beanie. Oh, yeah, Noor was also Wiccan, which is when you're into pagan matriarchy and cast spells instead of being Christian. Even Teta, who is super Catholic, was a bit into the Wiccan thing. She did read our coffee grounds, after all. Wicca is a very woman-positive religion, but I have to say, they dress horribly. Like last-minute cosplay outfits. Noor's Wiccan buddies wear velvet bodices and black lace gloves, but they also wear their transitions glasses with wire frames and, like, *scrunchies* in their hair. At least Noor was more of the graphic-T and combat-boot Wiccan. She really wanted a pentacle tattoo, but Mom said no, it was too expensive on top of our hydro bill.

You could never hear Noor's footsteps. Standing perfectly still is what she did for attention. She also affected a calm, blank expression when she interacted with people, which everyone thought was sweet, but I knew was a trap. She stood there in her oversized jeans and T-shirt, looking like an elf trying to pass as human, and dropped her eyes briefly to the crotch of my leggings. She flicked her eyes up again, her heavy black eyebrows slightly raised.

"I can see your labia," she said, grabbing an apple out of the bowl on the counter.

"Well, excuse my vagina!" I said.

"Vagina is on the inside!" she called as she left. I followed her outside where she stood looking at the boxes and bags I had piled on the garden path.

"Noor, don't you think we should use my university money to make the garage an off-the-grid safe house?" I asked her.

"I think you should invest in being an activist and showing up at the marches," said Noor. And she went up to her room.

Marches! That's the last thing I needed, being rounded up and put in pens or, worse, tear-gassed. I wasn't stupid. Mom had told me all about the G20 summit when all the world leaders came to Toronto and the protesters against the bad economy were "kettled" by the police, which means surrounded until they were bunched together and tear-gassed and pushed into cages in parking lots.

"They literally put us in a cage with no charges," said Mom.

Point taken.

I needed a vape. I couldn't vape in front of my parents, so I went out to our rotting front porch, my hands already searching in my fanny pack for the smooth yummy cylinder. I pulled it out and took a tight inhale. Aahhh. Okay. Apple Blossom. Breathe in and vapour out. So hard to believe the vapour wasn't smoke.

I looked out over my quiet street, scanning for possible sources of danger in case of natural disaster. Toronto had broken heat records the day before and random people without air conditioning were lining up outside the library across the street for some relief. It was drizzling a bit and a few cars swooshed wetly down the block, but the street was otherwise deserted. I leaned against the porch rail, which wobbled, and scanned my weather app.

I heard a phlegmy cough and Old Man Marco trundled by on his electric tricycle with the wagon on the back. The wagon was filled with antennas and old metal scraps. We deliberately didn't look at each other. I didn't like how he looked at me when I caught his eye. And I didn't like how he looked at me when I wasn't looking. His corpse of a house next door was an eyesore of steel junk and broken bicycles, which, I was beginning to realize, had lots of handy tools for a bunker situation. His front lawn was paved with concrete and covered in old metal fences and bits of pipe. He rarely spoke to anyone and looked cranky all the time. My mom, of course, was nice to him, sometimes bringing him green drinks that just seemed to confuse him, although he did leave scavenged houseplants on our front porch for her sometimes.

"He has congestive heart failure. He needs oxygen, really," Mom said when we were watching him wheeze and leaf-blow his concrete front lawn. "God forbid he should use a broom," she added. She was trying to get him to go to a clinic.

The metal tumbled out of Old Man Marco's wagon when he bumped into his driveway. I watched him scrabble around for a few seconds. Maybe he had the right idea, scavenging every day.

Our bottle-collection lady slowly pushed her clanking buggy down the street. A beardster in ear pods hustled behind her in a classic Toronto fastwalk, then clipped her shoulder when he passed. Fool. With the pods in, he'd never be able to hear the telephone poles and tree branches if they started falling. I looked up. Downed electricity lines would definitely be a problem, too. Once the power was out, you better believe the Toronto fastwalkers would be fastwalking towards other people's food and shelter. If the future was up to my parents and their generation, we were Mad Max doomed.

Survival Tip #5

Plants You Can Eat

The Universal Edibility Test

Wait about half an hour between steps. First, to find out if something is edible, smell it. If it smells okay, rub it on the inside of your elbow or wrist, and wait to see if you develop a reaction, like a rash. Then rub it on your lips. Then put some in your mouth and taste it, but don't swallow it. After that, your final step is to eat a small amount and wait overnight. If you don't get any digestive stress, you should be good to go.

> (I tried it with a random weed in the backyard, which tasted very bitter. But then I ruined it by having dinner. Not my fault we were having grape leaves.)

CHAPTER 5
Angels Are Real

Our street is not quite a neighbourhood or what planners like to call a community. It's really a residential offshoot of the sprawling Dufferin Mall two blocks away. The Dufferin Mall used to be a notorious and dingy gang hub and, even though it's been renovated and now has lots of brand-name fashion stuff, it still has that vibe. Like, it still has what Noor and I call the Sleazy Girlfriend Store that sells disposable club wear, the Trophy Wife Store that sells imitation designer sheath dresses and, for your final stage of womanhood, the Lady Store that sells boxy animal print suits and polyester lace mother-of-the bride outfits. Now the boys can get $200 sneakers at, like, four different places, and there are a gajillion cellphone kiosks. There is even a jewelry store for all your engagement and sexual coercion needs — lotsa heart-shaped stuff. Plus a discount grocery store and a Walmart, which you do *not* go to on a Saturday night. It's a scary place.

The streets all around the mall are a mix of ragged rooming houses, nice old Portuguese family homes with statues in gardens (and usually one jobless kid smoking on the porch) and other working poor like us. The neighbourhood has not gelled. There's now a thirty-three-story tower being built on the main intersection that has only increased the disconnected feeling.

We knew only the people two doors down on either side of us, although a newcomer German family, Mrs. Vogel and her son, had moved in across the street and there was a refugee house half a block down that was finally making it interesting around here. You can see the Syrians and Africans trundling their cheap suitcases up and down the street, bravely prepared to enter the subway, which lately had broken air conditioning even in the heat wave. After roasting in Jordanian refugee camps for a year, maybe the Toronto subway system in a heat wave didn't seem so bad, I dunno. They probably felt like the gun violence here, which was stupid gang boys of all backgrounds idiotically shooting each other in malls and clubs, was normal and nicely contained.

Dad translated for the Syrian newcomers and Mom ran an English conversation class once a week at the community centre where Teta went. Sometimes I helped with babysitting the kids.

At the top of our street is a brick low-rise with the Women's Centre on the ground floor, a resource and support centre for domestic live-ins. When I was ten, Women's Centre got a grant from the local arts council to install a garden in front of their cinder-block storefront. They painted a bright mosaic and installed concrete benches around a rock garden. In the middle of the rock garden they put up a life-size statue of a naked woman holding a planter. It was nice that the Centre ladies began to timidly enjoy their Tupperware lunches on the benches during the day, but the benches also became a hangout for drunk stragglers at night. Our evening lullabies became the faint shouts of those stragglers. You'd hear things like cracky female yells or the low laughter of men hiding their beer. And the Doppler effect of the skateboarders clattering down the street to the skate park, who were louder than airplanes overhead. Thanks, city planners, putting a skate park right at the end of my street! But I can't be too mad — I clattered down the street on skateboards with Desmond in my day (like, age twelve), too. Actually, it's not even young people on the skateboards anymore. I have to do a double take when I see bearded and grey-haired people zoom by. Old people with one great big calf.

I was actually skating by the Centre while they were raising the Statue of the Naked Lady four years ago. I was thirteen. I had to stop, kick up my board and stare. The construction workers looked uncomfortable handling the statue, especially when their fat yellow gloves grabbed and slapped her sides and pushed at the curved stone belly. The Lady was holding up a planter on her right shoulder. Her grey stone body looked kind of realistic, except, of course, the smooth crotch. Unfortunately, the sculptor had given her an old-fashioned hairdo, like a bad eighties perm. The workers were mostly young guys and trying to be respectful, but they also were trying not to laugh or meet each other's eye.

It was pretty funny, mostly because the stone lady's mild smile stayed the same no matter where the men's hands were. Mrs. Perez, the Woman's Centre office manager, was looking down at her clipboard, trying to seem like this was normal, like a nurse in the examining room when a big male doctor has to pap a virgin. I immediately thought, *OMG this is Noor territory*. I popped back on my board, scooted down the street to our house and bolted up the stairs into Noor's room.

"Noor, come on! You gotta see this! There's a naked lady statue on the street!"

Normally Noor was resistant to reacting in any way to me, I mean, she's acted like the older one since she was born two years after me. But this time the little sister flashed alive in her for, like, a millisecond, and she jumped up and followed me. Now that I know she's into naked ladies, it makes a little more sense. Mom heard us pounding back down the stairs.

"Unload the dishwasher — this is the last time!" she yelled from the couch. She had been heavily into a seven-season DVD binge for the past month. She was starting to look messed up for a naturopath, sort of bloated with dark circles under her eyes.

"Yeah!" we called, already out the front door. If you were visiting from another planet you would think "Unload the dishwasher this is the last time" was the normal greeting in our house. We skipped up the street and then stopped just before we got to the Centre. We wanted to look as if we were just casually walking by.

"Holy cow," whispered Noor as we slowed in front of the garden.

"Don't giggle," I said.

The men were holding the Statue of the Naked Lady sideways and slowly pushing her erect. When they got her up securely, they stood back, their expressions very professional. A worker began to gently arrange a heavy chain around one of the statue's slim ankles. The chain was attached to a rebar imbedded into the soil. So, like, now we were all looking at a naked lady chained to a piece of rebar.

"That's not a good look," I said.

"Looks good to me," said Noor.

Mrs. Perez glanced at us wearily. "Yes," she said, "the bushes, they will grow." She pointed at some potted purple-leafed plants on the ground.

Noor and I snuck over to visit the Naked Lady that night.

"She can be our guardian angel," said Noor, who got heavily into angels on her way to becoming a Wiccan.

We went home to the computer in the kitchen and tried to look up female guardian angels. Unfortunately, we went down an internet rabbit hole after searching "Can guardian angels fall in love?" The questions on the angel site, man. Noor and I almost peed ourselves laughing. It was one of those sister close times — leaning together into the computer, gripping each other's hands and laughing so hard we couldn't even look each other in the face, going "Stop! Stop!"

We searched "Are angels and fairies the same thing?"

And the *answer*!

"No, angels and fairies are not the same thing. Angels are real."

"Angels are real" became forever how we argued after that to shut someone down. Then we had to look up "Would an angel and human relationship ever really work?" Noor read from the angel website guy, an American Bible fundamentalist:

"The difference between a human and an angel is so extreme it would be hard to commune," intoned Noor in what I now call her Wise Woman voice. At the time, I thought it sounded like a very old-fashioned teacher. I started thinking of it as her Wise Woman voice a couple years ago when she was practising spells. "Angels have lived through millennia. They have seen the face of God and they understand far more than the human ever could. When you get to heaven, you love everyone with pure agape love."

Then we had to look up "agape love," which is the highest form of love, apparently. We couldn't find the name of any female guardian angels. Sexist heavenly bastards. We thought about calling her Angita, the roman goddess of witchcraft and healing, but truly we just ended up calling her the Statue of the Naked Lady.

Over the summer, a fuzzy purple bush did grow over the ankle chain, and then up to her knees, and then over her smooth pudendum. And finally, her breasts. The planter she held up spilled petunias. I got used to her. It was comforting that a naked woman could stand unmolested as high school students, drug dealers and library patrons passed by her like goldfish around coral. She gave a bit of glamour to the homeless people sheltering meekly on the benches. Most of our homeless were meek, like the Anishinaabe lady who is the only one I give money to. But there's also the skinny old man with the nicotine beard who tries to catch my eye and yell at me from Bloor Street doorways. He was like a violent gnome, yelling weirdly mean and personal things like, "Smile! You are a girl, you are supposed to be *happy*!" And once when I offered him a chocolate bar, he shook his head no and then shrieked after me, "Don't ever have babies. *Don't ever have babies*!"

Uh, I don't want to anyway, so . . .

The Statue of the Naked Lady came in handy when I started having climate change anxiety, since it started around the time the statue was erected. Honestly, I was still sometimes scared to cross Bloor Street, but the Lady was just far enough away from the house that I felt I could escape a little bit. When I annoyed my family with my anxiety, I sat on the bench and stared at her calm face, wishing I was made of stone, too. I hoped that, at least, by not being at home, something in life could happen to me apart from being scared all the time and no one caring. Anything else. For about six months the Lady comforted me because she was there, naked yet still safe. I imagined her saying, "Hello, Jamilah. How are you today? Don't worry, everything will be okay."

Then one day she was gone, leaving only the chain attached to the rebar lying on the ground. Stolen or escaped? My first instinct was to check Old Man Marco's backyard. He, for sure, had a huge chain cutter. Peering over the fence, I saw only the usual old BBQs and oil drums and garbage. After that, I still went to the bench to sit by the purple bush. But that's when I started unrolling the crushed cigarette butts I picked up from the ground and smoking them. I pretended the Lady had escaped.

Survival Tip #6

How to Survive in a Desert

- Remain calm: take deep breaths and collect your thoughts.

- Conserve energy: remain covered during the hottest part of the day. Move around when it's cooler.

- Find water: look for animals and plant life to follow. Dig a hole and wait for dew or moisture.

- Find cover: protect your head from the sun first. At night, rocks, backpacks and supplies can provide warmth.

- Stay away from dangerous wildlife: often bright markers on animals and insects denote danger. They are usually very shy, but stay away from them.

CHAPTER 6
It's Not the Heat, It's the Humanity

In the second week of the heat wave, it got so bad that the city opened cooling centres. It was so bad we were supposed to check on old people.

I hung out in my room watching my phone. I was lonely. Vivian had her job. Desmond was gaming. God, I was hot. The bunker would definitely need a generator for an AC unit. I went down the rabbit hole and started doomscrolling.

"Canada, the US and China biggest polluters!"

"Climate refugee crisis looming!"

"Tar sands, climate change deniers, fires, floods!"

There was a photo of an old newspaper, yellowing around the edges. "The time to act is now," it said.

Ha.

Then I got stuck on this site called What Could Kill You. It was clearly by an American guy because he kept recommending that we get machine guns. Oh, crap. I never thought about biological warfare, killer bacteria, nano-litter, robots and pole shifts. What the hell was a pole shift? I moved on, because the guy kept swearing like he was a bad guy in an R-rated movie or something. So boring.

I looked up generators on my phone again. Wow! There were portable generators, inverter generators, standby generators. Oh, look! There was one called Natural Generator. There were two ways it generated electricity: 1) through an included solar panel and 2) through a wind generator port. There was a battery pack that stored energy. It was quiet and wouldn't emit any toxic fumes. But it was like $2,000. No. Can't do that. To heck with the environment. I was going to have to get a portable gas-powered one. Or *we* were.

Sometimes Dad and I drank our coffee together in the living room and watched the news channel before he went to work. He liked the heat, unless the humidex got high. Then Dad always said, "Yes, it was hot in the old country, but not with this humidity."

The news channel was almost as mesmerizing as the weather channel. It had an upper right-hand rectangle with hourly temperatures that dissolved into five-day forecasts. It had a little square of talking heads on the left. It had live action and print ads. It had news slowly scrolling across the bottom bar. Often, the news scroll was especially horrifying because the text slowly revealed the death or abuse of a dog or a toddler, word by word. Super creepy. Dad would yell, "Dog!" or "Toddler!" so I could go "Agh!" and turn away in time. That day they were covering a protest of people living in tents at city hall. It looked like a bunch of younger people in colourful rags carrying weird signs like "Climate Rebellion" and "Climate Justice."

"Mass civil disobedience and disruption seem to be the goal of these eco-radicals," said a reporter with false eyelashes and intense contouring. "But so far, only thirty are in attendance and the police are allowing them to stay in their tents."

"This is not just an environmental problem," said a protester in a faded blue bandana, pajama pants and Doc Martens. "This is an existential problem."

I looked up "existential." It said "grounded in existence." I understood what the protester said less.

On the less-than-super-hot nights, I slept on Teta's couch under her paint-by-number scene of a French lady and her suitor simpering at each other. Teta often had really loud Egyptian TV on in the background. Egyptian TV is like tacky American TV, but it's not only talk-show people being super fake. It's Arabs trying to be white people being super fake, so basically it feels like watching a meta puppet show. I'll admit, once for a few weeks, Teta and I did get into an Egyptian weight-loss contest. It actually had ladies on treadmills in burkas. Seeing women in full burka coverage makes me very depressed. Teta, too. To us, they looked like portable prisons, not protection.

In a glass-fronted china cabinet, Teta has a picture of herself from when she was about twenty. She and her best friend Abla are in full beehive hairdos, sleeveless dresses and fake eyelashes. Abla, who was Muslim, is wearing a scarf loosely on her head, and her long hair and bangs are showing. Traditional Palestinian dress never had us in full veils or niqab. That came later, especially in Gaza by the sea. Since Israel was established in 1948, many Palestinians became more fundamentalist Muslim. I get it — sometimes you have to go hard on identity when you are being erased. It's just that now the moderate and extreme ones are fighting each other as well as fighting for our rights, so it's harder to protect ourselves. Another reason I don't like protests. Dad often made us watch news clips of Palestinian kids with rocks getting gunned down by the Israeli Military. No, thank you.

"Did God make mistake?" Teta would ask about why so many girls in Palestine have to hide themselves now. Many of her other girlfriends growing up in Haifa were Muslim or Jewish. They went to each other's weddings and to the same beauty salons, and the veil was optional. Personally, I think the hijab is cute. And in this anti-Muslim climate, super brave. Also, no more bad hair days.

43

One of the hot-day mornings we had to go volunteer at the community centre.

It was 9 a.m. and already humming hot outside. Teta stuffed me full of za'atar, eggs and coffee and I went upstairs to change. I pulled on my capri leggings (I couldn't wear bike shorts with the Syrian women) and a nice oversize T-shirt, clonked down the stairs and followed Teta out the door. Teta walked very slow but she could walk. She had gotten better at walking after I made her get New Balances instead of those plastic mules that made her feet bulge. She still wore her insanely patterned polyester housedress with the NBs, though. Shuffling beside her, already sweaty, I put my hair up in a messy topknot, which, thank God, was the thing. I looked down to double check I'd worn a bra and the T-shirt didn't have food stains on the chest. Shit. I had accidentally put on my "What the eff you looking at?" T-shirt from Noor's slut walk. We were almost there. Teta hadn't noticed yet so, quickly, I slipped the tee over my head, reversed it and pulled it down so it was on inside-out. At least I had a bra on, so I wasn't completely topless on the sidewalk.

"Eh," said Teta, "what you doing?"

"Oh," I said. "This is the style."

She squinted at the backwards, now faint, black letters on the tee. "This is style?" she asked.

"Yes," I said confidently.

An extremely loud plane buzzed overhead, practising for the damn air show that day. Damn it. Why is there always an air show in the city during a heat wave? Why can't they put it in a big empty space in the country? You'd think that, with all the times the pilots crashed into each other, it would finally end, let alone forcing people out of the city, shaking like chihuahuas. Darn Air Show.

We got to the beautifully over-air-conditioned community centre and went down to the basement kitchen. The linoleum floor and grey walls of the room were brightened up a little by the smell of parsley and mint. Three women, in their coloured and patterned head scarves (one was even wearing a gold lamé hijab), were making kibbeh and tabbouleh to cater a book-launch event. Three kids were sitting at a table, colouring, along with an older man who looked very sad. He nodded.

Teta went to the ladies and they all kissed both cheeks.

"*Helwe, Helwe*," they said to me, which means "beautiful." They all kissed me, too, and ran their hands up and down my arms. They were very handsy.

"Eh — a little big," said the oldest, most-wrinkled lady with a smile. The one with the gold lamé head scarf. There's always an old relative in Arabic culture who will tell you you are too fat. Always. Vivian says it's the exact same with her Jewish relatives. Must be a Semitic thing. Or a diaspora thing, where all us scattered people try to fit into white culture.

"Why are you having the war exercises?" one asked us after another plane thundered overhead.

Teta started into a bowl of shortbread dough, quickly making little round balls and putting holes in them with her thumb to stuff in a date squib. Her large, competent hands moved swiftly, hands that had taken care of families all her life. Married at fifteen, she would have been an apprentice housewife since she was a toddler, making and rolling and cutting and chopping and picking parsley. Arabic food is very time intensive. I personally suspect the women decided to make time-intensive food so they could sit around a table together and talk while the men worked.

The two young women were Mona and Asma. Mona had a sweet face and was the mother of Aziz, a handsome, skinny eleven-year-old boy with a slight mustache, and Leila, an eight-year-old in faded pink shorts with a sequined T-shirt. Asma was the mother of three-year-old Malik. Malik had a huge nose and buzzed hair that made him look like he had male-pattern baldness. Seriously, he looked like a tiny businessman. Asma wore an extremely high hijab to show off that she had a shit ton of hair underneath it. It was like a beehive hijab. She was made up like a drag queen. For all our modesty restrictions, we Arab ladies do not mind makeup. She was wearing a cheap sweater and skinny jeggings with Uggs and she looked *pissed*. She looked at me like she wanted to kill me. When I said hello, she sneered and looked away.

Mona took my arm and whispered, "It's okay she mad. Her brother lost last week in wars."

I immediately felt like piece of crap, so I walked over to where Asma was picking parsley and said what I thought she would like to hear. "*Helwe*," I said. "How do you get your eyebrows like that?"

She looked up at me briefly and gave me a small smile. It was more, I could see, for my sake than hers.

The older man at the table was doing nothing while the women cooked. He side-eyed my leggings, tapping one hand by an ashtray filled with empty pistachio shells. It's a tough culture shift for guys who used to be, like, Sharia-law-legislated king shit over women. He'd probably be a lot happier if he just adjusted and started babysitting and cooking (my dad cooked a lot) instead.

My job was to take care of the three kids.

"Uhm, you wanna go to the park?" I asked. "They have a kiddie pool."

The kids watched me calmly, not even trying to be nicey nice. I guess if you've been in a refugee camp for a year and nearly die in smuggler boats, you don't feel you have to be fake nice to everyone.

"I must ask," said Aziz, and he did.

Mona's response in Arabic was obviously, "I don't care. Just get out so I can have some peace."

Asma pointed to a diaper bag and Leila grabbed it.

"I just have to go to the bathroom," I said, and slipped away. I grabbed two rolls of the grey toilet paper and put it in my bag for the bunker.

"Okay," I said, walking out. "Let's go!"

We left the community centre and walked along the hot sidewalk back to the park, Malik holding my hand. Now, normally when I'm with children, I apply the just-make-sure-they-don't-die approach and avoid that whole talking-in-a-high-pitched-voice, peek-a-boo-and-bedtime-story routine. But these guys needed special treatment. Also, I felt a little self-conscious making them walk in a heat wave in unfamiliar territory with a stranger. Was this triggering them? Would one of them cry?

"So," I said too clearly. "Can you help me count to ten in Arabic, Malik?"

"Maaalik," he corrected me.

"Maleek," I said.

"*La la*," he said shaking his head ("No no"). "Maaalik." He was irritated with my stupidity. His mouth was turning down. This kid had a temper.

"Maleek," I tried. I couldn't help it if Syrian and Palestinian dialects were different. Plus, I was totally not at all fluent. There was that.

"Laaaaaaa!" he wailed and suddenly plonked his diaper butt on the sidewalk. Oh, no, God, it happened, I had triggered the poor thing. Leila, who was clearly the mother-in-training, went over and picked him up. We had to move along more slowly to match her pace. Aziz was being cool. Placating infants was beneath him. His eyes were straight ahead and roving the landscape, narrowing when they saw a bicycle, so he was okay. Lily was stumbling under Malik's weight. Oh, God. I was going to have to carry him and I was going to have to go "gaga googoo" to make him let me carry him. It looked like Malik set the tone for everyone in the room. He was probably going to be a great leader someday. I'm sure brilliant little Gandhi was a pain in the butt at that age, too. I mean, he became a lawyer. A British lawyer. Pain. In. The. Butt. (Forgive me, Allamudeen, for I have sinned.)

"One!" I said super-fake happy, putting a finger in Malik's face.

There was a faint rumbling like a large truck rolling by, then suddenly a warplane screamed overhead and ripped the oxygen out of the sky. I almost had a heart attack. But Malik didn't even flinch. He smiled, his face transforming into Mr. Adorable.

"One!" he said back, a baby finger pointing up.

Okay.

We got to the park.

Mom says the neighbourhood is getting more gentrified, which is when you get microbreweries and coffee shops. It's true that the street people who hang by the restroom building in the park were starting to look like they felt a bit out of place beside the millennials throwing their blankets on the urine-crunchy grass (I would say the urine was just from the dogs, but I also see men pissing here in broad daylight) or playing Ping-Pong at the concrete Ping-Pong table and buying and selling at the organic market. The park is only about two blocks squared, but it still managed to include an ice rink that is a skate park in the summer, one rolling hill and a playground. Maybe the Toys R Us in the mall makes donations, because there are always plastic toy trucks and dolls lying on the ground. As we walked onto the yellow grass, Malik just stopped and stood perfectly still in front of a fat, red, plastic toy dump truck.

He looked up at me.

"Yes," I said, "you can touch it. It's for everyone."

He fell on it. Leila and Aziz waited patiently. Their job was to indulge the baby boy. Their bodies were very still, but their eyes were scanning the park, registering the thin white yoga moms and their fat toddlers. I could feel the envy coming off them. I went over and handed Leila my sunglasses. She smiled, put them on and instantly posed like an Instagram model — hip out, hand on her pink polyester shorts, her cheap T-shirt decal sparkling.

"Take picture," she said.

I pulled out my battered Android. I took a picture and showed it to her. She jumped up and down and giggled and smiled. Oh, God, it had already started. I should introduce her to Vivian.

Survival Tip #7

How to Make a Fire

For every method, build a tinder nest of stuff that catches fire easily, like dry grass, leaves and bark.

(Yes, this is the origin of Tinder. It starts fires, get it? So corny, I know.)

- **Traditional: angle a lens towards the sun until a beam of light sets the tinder on fire.**

- **Battery and steel wool: rub the battery on the steel wool until it glows. Transfer the burning wool to your tinder nest.**

- **Waterproof matches: put a thin layer of clear nail polish on them and let them dry. Then, even if your canoe tips, they will light!**

(I totally got into doing this and used them to light dried leaves, and almost melted one of Noor's fairy gardens. One of the fairies has a melted wing now.)

- **Friction-based fire.**

(That's when you rub sticks. Impossible.)

CHAPTER 7
Bloom Where You Are Planted

The kids didn't even seem to notice the blazing sun and the heat as they played. As usual, the humidity made my eyelids feel greasy and made me grip my lips as I tried to stand in the one bit of shade under a thin tree. My skin seemed to sizzle within seconds of the sunlight hitting it. Has anyone else noticed the sun is hotter these days?

The screams and squeaks of the Dufferin buses twenty metres away did not help the general sweatshop feeling. Then I felt and heard a slow, low rumbling and looked up. The rumbling accelerated into a scream that tore through the air. I crouched like I had been smacked by a giant hand, my arms up. Another evil, pointy-nosed war jet.

Car alarms went off and I quickly looked at Aziz, then Leila, to see if they were bothered by it. Nope, they were crouched down beside Malik and his toy truck. They didn't even look up. I didn't know if that was good or very, very bad.

I had heard about the Syrian refugee camps, of course. There was a civil war and Canada let in about 25,000 Syrians of the millions who were escaping. Dad and I watched a news story about how they travelled. So I knew there was a lot of walking and some boats where people drowned. I knew they hid in containers and even took taxis. I guess, like the kids in Gaza, these Syrian kids grew up with bombs and houses falling around them. So I felt I should distract them. Maybe the mud pit.

There was a mud pit in a corner of the park — literally a plot of mud with a pipe gushing water in the middle. You would go in it to build rivers and stuff. Then you would float things down your little rivers and you get gloriously covered in mud. I used to take George to it when he was little until one day he walked away scowling and said, "It's like a mean fighting" because a kid had crushed his dam and built his own river.

"You want to go in the mud pit?" I asked. Leila looked disdainful and Malik looked scared. Oh, yeah. Damn. I couldn't get anything right. Their refugee camp must have been a mud pit. That's what scared them. Next to the mud pit was the round concrete wading pool, though. Fresh, bright blue and cool-looking. Malik clenched his fists and actually trembled when he saw the water. So we took off his pants and T-shirt, leaving him naked except for his saggy disposable diaper.

"Can he go in like this?" I asked the lifeguard.

"Sure," the lifeguard said. So Malik went in with just his diaper, which, yes, was disgusting. He was making everyone swim in his butt juice. But he was also so joyful, all pink and brave with his little chest out, and his "can you believe this?" smile clocking everybody, like he had just won the World Cup. Even the lifeguard and the yoga moms smiled at him. He reminded me of a phrase Mom always said: "Bloom where you are planted." For a second, I wished I was as brave as this little kid. Or even as brave as my dad, coming to Canada to start a new life. The pool's blue-painted bottom against the white border gave the effect of a tropical beach. But the water must have been filthy, even with the urine and the chlorine keeping everything basically sterile, unless that particular combo started creating a toxic gas.

Malik immediately began to pick up floating plastic balls and throwing them at a boat, turning to me and squealing each time. There were a lot of toys floating in the pool. Bobbing next to him was a spongy, skin-coloured object that looked dirty. I looked closer. Oh, it was a cloth doll, face down and without clothes. Its head and extremities were plastic, so its little hands bobbed over the sunken body. I just kinda stared at it for a few seconds. It was extra-gross for some reason, maybe because the wet canvas body was streaked with dark grey and the stitching looked like it would hurt. Oh, shit, it was extra gross because it looked exactly like a dead baby floating beside little Malik. I looked up at the lifeguard who was standing a few feet away.

"Hey," I hissed, trying not to be obvious with my hand gestures.

"Oh, shit," he said and snatched it up.

Malik's lips were turning blue anyway, so I grabbed his hand and hustled him out of the pool. We had another two hours before we could go back to the community centre. I decided we should walk the two blocks up to my house and just watch TV.

This turned out to be the hardest part of the day. We were all tired and soggy. It's not a short walk for kids already tired from the heat and the park. It was now around 2 p.m., that maddening time of the day where there is no shade on my road at all. Usually there's at least one side of the street you can get shade on, but now we were looking at being on the baking bright concrete and under the sun for ten minutes straight.

"Okay," I said. "Let's go. We can have lemonade when we get to my house."

"You have Coke?" asked Aziz.

We walked for about five minutes. I felt worried about their small, thin shoulders and knees under that sun. I felt worried they were always walking in someone else's control. Was this hurting them? Doubling down on trauma? Malik started to whine. I went to

53

pick him up but he recoiled, sat down on the sidewalk and dropped his head like a tired old man.

A squadron of triangular-shaped planes split the sky again. Malik looked up and this time he did scream. Because this time he saw them. Leila, really not much bigger, had to hoist him up, his legs around her torso. We continued to walk, super slow, like ants under a magnifying glass. Finally, we dragged ourselves onto my porch and they collapsed into the wicker chairs.

"Living room," I said, thinking of the blessed, blessed, babysitting superpowers of the TV.

We went inside and Leila dumped Malik on Dad's fat brown rocker La-Z-Boy. He perked up immediately at its movement. I turned on the TV. It was tuned to SpongeBob. I, myself, found the cartoon weirdly creepy and off-putting. There was something nauseating about the shaky line drawings of the sea creature's bits and bobs. But maybe the kids didn't notice.

I went to the kitchen. There was no Coke, of course, just mango nectar and stevia ginger ale. Stevia pop is disgusting. Even if stevia is an herbal sweetener, it still manages to taste exactly like aluminum to me. So, mango nectar on ice, it is. Kids like ice more than anything anyway. I heard a crash and ran into the living room to see Malik standing on the La-Z-Boy backwards and rocking violently. The side-table lamp was on the floor, its lampshade indecently tilted. The bulb had not broken, at least. Leila and Aziz were sitting on the couch, looking at the TV.

"Please turn off," said Aziz, gesturing to the TV. Was it the unaccustomed noise? Or was he protecting the little ones from the vulgarity? SpongeBob was pretty wretched — he was currently pulling off his pants and farting.

I turned off the TV. I gave them their drinks. Malik took his and right away started trickling it on the carpet, his eyes straight on me. I needed backup.

"Noor!" I yelled up the stairs.

Pause.

"Noor!"

"What?" she called down faintly.

"Bring me the Barbie Box!"

No answer. Dammit, I had made the mistake of sounding like I was giving her a command. You could not give Noor commands. She was very sensitive about that.

"Sorry, Noor. Noor, *habibti*," I said, calling her "my love." "Please help. I can't leave the kids alone."

No answer.

I didn't dare run upstairs. Malik had just jumped off the wildly rocking La-Z-Boy and was now crouched by the fireplace, shoving a fist into the ashes. Aziz was leaning back on the couch openly smirking. Shit! I ran to the kitchen, grabbed a dishtowel and tried to clean Malik's hands. He began to wail at the indignity.

"You come up!" yelled Noor.

"I can't! I can't leave the kids. I'm babysitting. Please bring the Barbie Box!"

"Arright, arright . . . jeez."

A few minutes later, Noor came down holding a cardboard box. It was our secret stash of dollar store "fashion dolls" left over from her grade six art project. For the project, she had glued ten fashion-doll heads to a canvas, each floating over a tiny, hand-crocheted niqab she had made. This is where Noor leaves us all behind. Was it a statement against the niqab, showing you shouldn't force a human to hide their face? Or was it a statement for the niqab, where underneath them everyone has dignity and stuff? Personally, I think it looked a little serial-killer-y. But we kept the dolls, hid them from our mom (who wouldn't let us have them growing up because they perpetuated bad body images) and secretly designed clothes for them out of our old T-shirts.

"Here," she said, and dumped the contents of the box on the coffee table. Tiny plastic body parts and torsos fell out amongst the bright fabric scraps.

"Hey." She nodded to the kids. They totally changed, sullenness gone, alert and bright as they looked at her. They knew quality when they saw it. Noor's head was shaved and she was wearing a crop top, no bra and men's pleated pants belted tightly at the waist. Malik staggered to her and threw his arms around her legs.

"This is Noor!" I said. *Please stay, please stay*, I thought, trying to mind control her.

"Yeah, hi," said Noor. She smiled down at Malik and gently pushed him away. He was happy just to be touched by her. Noor's eyes narrowed at me. "Is that my T-shirt? Wash it."

Then she turned and walked back up the stairs. The window on the landing briefly created a haloed silhouette around her bald head as she passed by it. Bloody Noor. Malik tried to follow her, but I grabbed him and turned him to the Barbie Box. I managed to get a half-dressed full-limbed doll in his hand before he could start yelling.

Aziz, disgusted once again, leafed through a *Mother Jones* magazine, but Leila leaped on the doll clothes and started sorting them. Malik circled the room holding the Barbie like a club and hit everything he could.

Aziz looked out the back window and saw the broken bikes and boxes strewn around. He turned to me eagerly for the first time. "You have bikes shop?" he asked.

"Well, they are all broken."

"I can fix them. Can I go?"

"Sure."

He spoke briefly to the other kids in Arabic and they ran to the window.

"C'mon," I said.

We all went out to the backyard. Malik got on the old pink tricycle of Noor's, while Aziz expertly turned a bike upside down and fiddled with the chain, Leila walked up to the garage and looked in.

"I'm turning this into a special safe room," I told her. "In case of emergency."

"You really have to clean," she said. "Ours was very clean." She looked around. "You need more water."

Survival Tip #8

What to Do in a Blackout

- You can't depend on your phone, so write down important contact phone numbers like hospitals and friends and relatives.

- Switch phone to power save.

- Use gas BBQs to cook food that will spoil.

- Unplug appliances to avoid a surge when power comes on.

- Check on neighbours, especially the elderly and sick.

- Keep generator as far away from house as possible and watch for carbon monoxide poisoning if it is fuel-powered.

  (The first thing I think about is people on life support. But guess what. Hospitals have *generators*!)

CHAPTER 8
Blackout

Finally, someone understood the bunker! We hunted for tools for Aziz to fix the bicycles and swept up a little, and then it was time to go. I took the kids back to the community centre, and it was better than the walk to my place. Aziz had gotten Dad's old ten-speed bike working and let his sister take turns riding it on the way back. Malik happily rode the tricycle. When we got to the community centre kitchen, all the kids ran to their moms talking excitedly about the bikes. I followed, carrying the tricycle.

"Malik can keep this tricycle," I said to Asma. "If that's okay."

Asma regally accepted. The other women kissed my face and held my hands.

"*Shukrun!*" they said. "Thank you. How nice."

I went home with Teta, walking Dad's bike, then went to my room. Emptying my backpack and looking at the day's bunker haul, I was disappointed. Just the two toilet paper rolls. I put the toilet paper in the closet. I still needed a lot more canned goods and batteries. And I really wasn't going to relax until I got a crank radio, one that worked by turning a crank on its side, no electricity required. Canadian Tire had one for forty-nine dollars.

I turned on the AC unit and realized I had forgotten to

vape the whole time I was with the kids. I pulled out the vape and took a hit. I stared out my window. It was so hot the leaves were not moving and even the birds were holding their breath. When cars drove by, the sun bouncing off them was like laser beams. I saw a glint of something on the roof across the street, where Mrs. Vogel and her son had moved in. She was a small woman with a beige bowl cut and a dorky, beige kid. I often saw them buying crafts in the dollar store before I boycotted it because, you know, China climate change violations. Mrs. Vogel's house was plain. She kept her windows undressed and her porch bare. The top bedroom window framed only the back of a wood chair. Their house was so uncluttered you could see straight through the front living room window to the backyard. I didn't know if there was a dad. He would probably be too much clutter. Oh, wow. She had a solar panel on her roof! I wanted a solar panel. Maybe I could ask her about it.

I idly looked at YouTube. Yessss. A lady talk show. They were so dinky and the ladies were wearing so much makeup it was like they were in one of Teta's eighties Egyptian soap operas. Their wigs and weaves were out of control and they had little forced lady smiles on their faces. I loved watching those with Noor and just crapping on the total genderized dumbness.

"Noor!" I called, walking over to her room. She was sitting on her mattress on the floor with a sketchbook, a small fan slightly ruffling the muslin curtains. She was drawing intricate mandalas. She was in a minimalist stage, so all her possessions were in cardboard boxes under the window and there was just a bare lamp on the floor beside her. She was insanely composed in the heat. Probably because she was the size of a bird.

"Come into my room and watch Ladytalk with me!" Ladytalk was our nickname for all the daytime talk shows.

"No, it's too cold in your room."

"Come on, it is not too cold. You're too skinny. Wear a sweater."

"It's too loud. You have to make it too loud over the AC."

I left and went back to my room. The AC was nicely cooling it down anyway. I could almost forget the horrible, hissing, sizzling day outside.

Then — *VROOP* — the AC stopped. Shit! Yikes?

"Nooor!"

"What?"

"The power went out!"

I got out of bed and opened my door. The swamp heat of the hallway hit me like a wall. I went to Noor's room.

"The power went out," I repeated.

"So?" She was lying on her side, still tracing in her sketchbook. The fan was off. She didn't look up.

"Check your phone," I said.

"Oh, yeah." She glanced down. "Oh, battery's dead."

I went back to my room to check my phone. I typed in "blackout."

"Major blackout affecting Greater Toronto Area."

No No *No. No!* Shit.

"OMG, it's happening!" I yelled.

"Relax," said Noor.

We heard George yelling in agony at the downstairs TV.

I got a text from Mom. *Blackout here you?*

I texted back, *70% of Toronto without power. Come home.*

On our way.

It was three in the afternoon and we had hours and hours and hours of intense heat coming. Already, the back of my neck was wet and my bra was suction-cupping against my ribs. I felt frightened. I went down to Teta's basement and tried to read

61

her *National Geographic*s by the recessed window light until Mom and Dad came home. Curled up on her scratchy couch, I suddenly felt a lower abdomen pang. Damn. My period. I went to the upstairs bathroom and put in a tampon. As soon as the blood started flowing, a bit of my edgy panic disappeared. Annoying hormones.

"Kids!" yelled Mom when she came in.

I jumped up the stairs two at a time. Mom was in a yellow cotton peasant blouse. Her face was red and her hair was almost twice its usual size. I went to the fridge.

"Don't break the seal!" Dad said. "If the power outage lasts longer than eight hours, our food will be ruined. We will have to cook the meat."

"I told you we need a generator," I said.

There was a knock and we all went to the front door. It was Peter and Barb, the nice couple who lived next door.

"Is your power out?" they asked.

"Yup," we said.

"Here," said Peter. "I have a crank radio. We can listen to the news."

Peter held out a four-by-six-inch black box radio. Awesome!

"Hey, I was just thinking I wanted one of those!" I said.

"Oh, yeah," said Peter. "It's great. Got it at Lee Valley. It can charge a phone, too."

We found an AM station that was running. "Strain on the transmission lines due to the heat wave and our outdated power infrastructure has caused a power outage in most of Metro Toronto," the radio said.

We were standing around the radio, looking down. Minutes before, we were each alone, looking down at our individual phones. Ten minutes without power and we were already primitive human beings in a circle looking at, basically, a campfire. I mentally put "firepit" on my list for the bunker.

Survival Tip #9

What to Do in Case of a Raccoon Attack

Raccoons are generally afraid of people, but they can carry rabies. Clap your hands, yell at the raccoon and step towards it — that should be enough to convince it to run off. You can also throw something or spray water on them. If you do get bitten or scratched by a raccoon, you should contact your family doctor immediately.

(Last year, raccoons had babies in our garage roof. They were fearless and cheerful but, like, not good. Once Dad half-heartedly tried to discourage them by spraying them with the hose, but they just stood up on the eaves and turned around and flipped over each other like kids playing in a sprinkler. Now we live with them.)

CHAPTER 9
Just a Theory

A few hours later, I was in the backyard squished into a plastic lawn chair. I could see through the chain-link fence that Old Man Marco had a few metal boxes and bowls lying around his hoarding back-yard that would make a great firepit. The temperature was still forty degrees. When the sun hit my skin, I felt seared.

Dad had his huge BBQ going. Peter and Barb brought some chicken and Mom brought out the seitan hot dogs. I tried to eat a dog, but when I squeezed the mustard I got that clear mustard pre-ejaculate that just makes the bun wet. That grossed me out so much, all I could eat was plain hot dog buns from the bag, piece by piece, just to settle my stomach. The white bread went gummy and stuck to my teeth. Plus, after two bites, I could pick up the chemicals in it, like a whiff of aluminum on the roof of my mouth. George did not have that problem. He was on his third dog.

I looked around, wondering what we had of value for the onset of a barter system when civilization died. Aunt Lily limped up to the house, dangling her heels in her hand. The subway was down and she had walked all the way from her downtown office. Her feet were bloody. Her dyed black hair was wet at the back, but her liquid black eyeliner was perfect.

"Give. Me. Booze," she said, and slumped on a lawn chair. I love Aunt Lily, but there was no good use for a lifestyle columnist in a barter system. Aunt Lily might have to go.

"A glass of wine?" I asked her.

"Yes, beautiful, thanks."

I went to the kitchen and grabbed a glass. Who's kidding who? I brought the whole bottle to her.

"Sit beside me," she said.

"No, I can't. There's no shade."

I leaned against the tree where a tiny bit of shade cut through the heat by about one-fifth of a degree.

"Honey, don't squint at the sun like that," she said while pouring the wine into the glass between her legs. "You'll get brown. Aren't you hot in those leggings? Go change."

Lily, Dad's sister, was one of those weirdly emancipated Arab ladies who were on their own personal crusade to make us all look white and thin in order to survive. She gave me red lipstick every Christmas. I mean, I was white-passing in the face, but these thighs do not lie. Aunt Lily also dressed for church in tight dresses, spike heels, fishnets and a blowout. Once I wore a long denim skirt and tunic, and she said, "Oh, you look like an Israeli girl." She did love when I rocked heavy eyeliner and big earrings and a kaffiyeh (the black-and-white-checked Palestinian scarf).

To be honest, I *was* hot in what I was wearing, plus I had period swamp crotch. I slumped back into the house and up to my room. The windows were still shut, but the stale air was morphing into the smell of moldy AC. I stripped off my leggings and went to put on my jean shorts. Oh, they were a bit tight. I put on boxer shorts and a strappy baby-doll dress that floated from my ribs comfortably. It was a bit booby. Leftover pre-period bloat, I guess. I went back downstairs and hung out the back screen door. It was getting darker.

"I'm going to go to Desmond's," I yelled. Desmond's parents are doctors. They were in Quebec for the summer, as usual, so he was at home alone. Being in his house was sort of like being in a huge operating room, because it's all decorated in white and chrome. The whole place would get really cold with the central AC on, especially the basement, so it was probably still cool there even with the blackout.

"Be careful," called Mom. "There are no street lights."

I walked by Old Man Marco's house with my eyes down. He was in a plastic chair on his porch, watching the undone world with satisfaction. *Try welding something now,* I hissed in my brain, feeling self-conscious in my booby top. I briefly fantasized about a spark from his OCD welding igniting his new oxygen tank. Bad karma, my mom would say. I was going to have to do a good thing now, like bring him food or something.

I went up to and along Bloor. Eight p.m. and the stupid sun was still blasting on the horizon. Shirtless cyclists caromed on the streets. They were the top of the transit food chain now. Subway refugees were still walking on the sidewalks, dazed and embarrassed, like they felt shy to even be seen in the same boat as everyone else. Like, how can we compete with each other now? People say Torontonians are cold, but I think we are just shy. Admittedly, the shyness is a bit exhausting and I hope it gets better with more newcomers coming in.

I turned onto Desmond's street, which has bigger detached houses. I swear the air got cooler just from more money. I went in through his side door and down to the basement and, as always, found Desmond in his tent on the indoor-outdoor rug. Yes, he slept in a tent. Inside.

"Uhm, are candles safe in a tent?" I asked, crawling in. It smelled of Doritos and old swampy bong water. He looked up at me, briefly annoyed, banging at a key on the computer on his lap.

"Shit, shit," he said. "I was just about to recharge."

"Are your parents at the cottage?" I asked.

"Yeah, they called. They're in Quebec, so they didn't know about it."

He put the computer down and lit a cigarette.

"Ugh," I said. "At least let's go outside."

"Get used to it, man," he said when we were in the driveway, listening to the calm air. "This is just a practice run."

"What do you mean?"

"This is all organized by the government," he said. "The secret government that runs the government."

"Oh, come on."

"No, man." Oh, no, he was going to start shouting. "In the next few years none of us are going to have any power. We will suffocate in the unflushed shit of the condos! It will be anarchy!"

"Has this got anything to do with 9/11?" I asked.

"It's the same people, but no. Look, I'll show you." He turned to go back inside and get his laptop. "Oh, yeah, no power," he said. "You know what we need? We need to get that generator set up. It's crazy that every house doesn't have one."

"I know," I said. "I asked for one for my seventeenth birthday instead of extensions."

He suddenly focused on me, eyes scanning me up and down. I felt self-conscious. It is so hard to dress when you get bloaty. It's like you're always accidentally falling out of your clothes.

"Wait," he said. "Are you, like, in a nightie?"

"Come on, let's go to my place," I said. "At least there's food."

I stalked away.

He danced around me, laughing. "Nightie! I like your nightie!"

I swatted him away. He wasn't even high.

We walked back into the steamy, now darkening Bloor Street evening. The corner stores were giving away ice cream.

Neighbours I've never seen before were chatting to one another, flashlights in hand.

"Listen," he said. "I want you to come to the Climate Change March next week in Ottawa. Road trip!"

"You know how I feel about marches," I said.

"I'll be there to protect you!" he said. "If I can do it, you can do it. And it's harder for me to protest. I'm more likely to get arrested and hurt."

I knew he was right. I felt a little ashamed of myself. My white-passing looks would probably protect him.

"We got to let the government know they can't get away with all this racist climate stuff," he insisted. "Jamilah, there's so many people now. Millions around the world. The government can't ignore us anymore."

Then he did something he had never done before. He took my hand and looked me straight in the eye. "We can go together," he said. "It could be like a getaway."

"You mean like a date?" I asked.

"Well, no . . . uhm, yes?" he stammered. "I mean, we don't have to do anything. I can drive and we can get an Airbnb and we can just, you know, hang."

"Okay," I said.

I trusted Desmond. I mean, I was still outfitting the bunker but, yes, it would be good to get over my march paranoia. We kept walking, now truly holding hands. I pictured our drive, and being alone together in an Airbnb (if we could get one). Yes. I definitely wanted to go to the Climate Change March with Desmond.

"Look," I said to change the subject as we walked by Mrs. Vogel's house, "she has solar panels."

The porch light was on. It was the only light on the street.

"Ahhh!" said Desmond and stood stock-still. I waited while

he stared at the house for a full minute. Then he nodded to himself. That's how Desmond processed. He had super concentration when he needed it.

We could hear the laughing in my backyard as we went up towards the house. Desmond went right to the grill and got three burgers.

Mrs. Vogel was there, talking to Aunt Lily, apparently about herbs. Her boy was playing in one of Noor's fairy gardens at her feet.

"The Greek oregano is fantastic," she was saying. "It grows on the mountains and it gets the minerals, you see."

I went up to them. "Hi," I said. "Those solar panels are so cool!"

Desmond ran up. "You have lights?" he asked her eagerly. "From the solar?"

"Solar power, yes," she said. "I run a business. It's called NRG Renew."

"Where do you store the energy?" asked Desmond.

"We have a battery in the basement connected to the panels."

"What happens when you run out?"

"An inverter automatically switches to the generator."

"Where did you get the generator?" I asked.

Mrs. Vogel gave me a quick look and then, I felt, went back to addressing Desmond.

"You should apply," she said to Desmond. Why wasn't she saying it to me? "We need workers this summer to help scout for clients. You get to use drones."

"Drones?"

"Yah, to scout for neighbourhoods for good places for the panels to go," she explained.

"Hey, what if I want to do it?" I asked.

"Let me see if there is something for you," said Mrs. Vogel.

I knew what "let me see" meant.

"You don't want to do that," said Mom. "It's hot, dirty work."

"I can do it!" I said. "I'm strong. I'm rebuilding the garage!"

I felt defensive. They never said "You don't want to do that" to Noor. Maybe it was because Noor just quietly did whatever she wanted and I had to talk about everything. Or maybe it was because I was the oldest girl, so I had to get all the old-country prejudice. The oldest kid in every immigrant family has to break in the parents. Also, Mom and Dad were, frankly, afraid of Noor.

"Mom," I said, changing the subject irritably. "I have made a decision."

"Oh, really," said Mom.

"I want to attend the Climate Change March in Ottawa next week."

"That's unlike you," said Mom. "Are you going to go on the bus with Noor and Beth?"

"No," I said. "Desmond will drive."

"Hmmm," she said. "We'll discuss this later, honey, okay?"

Well, her reaction could have been worse. Desmond and I backed off.

"Let's get a drink," I said to him.

I wasn't allowed to drink, but I was mad at the way Mrs. Vogel and Mom had brushed me off. I knew Dad kept a bottle of gin behind the cereal boxes over the fridge. He never drank it, but he always had it in the house because he thought it was classy, like you're in an old British movie wearing safari clothes after a long day of taming "the natives" in the hot sun. All that creepy British *Lawrence of Arabia* vibe. I grabbed a flashlight and Desmond and I went into the dim, hot kitchen through the back door. We found two reusable water bottles and filled them up with the gin. Looking back, that was probably not the best move.

By the time we got back outside, the women were smoking

(Mom hadn't smoked in *years*!) and drinking red wine around the picnic table. And the men were man-spreading in lawn chairs off to the side. Desmond and I planted ourselves under the lilac tree, sipping and wincing at the harsh, clear liquor. The candles were becoming inadequate and, without street lights, it was getting quite black in the sky.

I watched as Noor and Beth created some kinda Wiccan circle with twigs around a candle on a bare patch of the lawn.

"Hey, watch out — witches. Baby sacrifice zone," I whispered to Desmond.

He snorted. "Hey," he said. "Raccoons."

Three raccoons were starting to tiptoe around the picnic table and were spotted by Mom, Aunt Lily and Mrs. Vogel. Mom goo goo gaga-ed at them and they sat up and cocked their heads. All the ladies squealed. It was disgusting, really, all this repressed maternal need.

"Get out!" hissed Desmond to the raccoons. "Noor will sacrifice you!"

"Save yourselves," I said, and we started giggling.

Noor looked straight at us.

"Would you fools shut up?" she said.

One raccoon started eating bread from Mom's hand, another pushed his little leathery fist into an empty wine bottle on the ground.

"Look at us," said Aunt Lily. "Women trying to get rid of our love to helpless creatures who don't want us."

Something caught my eye in the back of the yard. It was a low, waddling skunk picking its way through the raspberry bush. It faded into the black shadows and we sat in its acrid wake.

"I like skunk smell," I said.

"Me, too," Desmond said.

I looked at the side of his face.

"It smells like weed."

I grabbed him by the shoulders and faced him square. "I don't like when you smell like weed," I said.

He looked surprised, then hurt. I let him go and leaned into him for a second. The place where his shoulder met his neck fit good. I rested there. He relaxed. He smiled. I liked his face when he smiled like that. He looked older. Probably prematurely aging from the weed. Mosquitoes started floating around. Gentle slaps began to keep time with the murmuring voices.

"The bats are dying of white-nose fungus," I heard Mom say.

"They are not controlling the mosquitoes anymore," said Mrs. Vogel. "At least your pond is not stagnant water."

"Yes, but," Mom leaned in, "the next-door guy has barrels of stagnant water and old pots filled with water and everything. It's a nightmare."

We heard Old Man Marco drop a lead pipe next door. He made noise whenever you said his name, like an offstage demon.

Our solar-powered pond pump (thank you, Lee Valley) was weakly sputtering, like someone whistling to look innocent. You couldn't blame it for feeling guilty. It *was* pretty stagnant, basically a mosquito condo. Shit. I could feel swamp crotch again. Any blood not quietly being absorbed by the tampon was now rappelling down the string into the crotch of my boxer shorts.

"The smoke is sacred, the tobacco is sacred, the wine is Dionysian," I heard Noor murmuring in her Wise Woman voice.

My phone pinged. It was a text from Vivian:

Blackout party at Marley's

Survival Tip #10

How to Survive a Zombie Attack

- **To identify a zombie, look for hunger for human flesh, open wounds and stiff gait.**

  (Okay, so basically Marley after a hockey game.)

- **Get a gun.**

  (What? Get a gun?! I checked the site. Oh, okay. It was American. Wow, did I want to learn how to shoot? Were there even shooting ranges in Toronto? Are all the gang kids going to end up becoming united and being our heroes?)

- **Always keep a can of gasoline on hand. Zombies can also be killed by fire.**

- **Look for secure, safe hiding spots, like abandoned buildings and get to know their entrance and exit ways. Keep an eye out for and outfit strategic shelters.**

  (On it.)

- **Keep quiet about it. Don't tell everyone about your prepping. If everyone crowds into your shelter, you'll all die.**

  (Well, that ship has sailed.)

CHAPTER 10
The Party

I ran upstairs, quickly changed my tampon and grabbed my go bag.

"Mom! Dad! Desmond and I are going to Marley's. Is that okay?" I asked on the way through the house.

"Be back at ten," said Dad. "Desmond, do not let her walk alone! There might be looters."

"I won't, Mr. Mansour," said Desmond.

"Do not let me walk alone," I muttered as we walked. "I wish I was, like, a superhero and everybody knew it. I could protect myself and everyone around me."

"You kinda are," said Desmond. "You're kinda being a superhero building the bunker and doing all this survival research."

"Right?" I affirmed. "I don't get no respect."

"Right. Like Wonder Woman except not wearing a bathing suit all the time."

"Yeah, what's up with that?" I asked. We laughed.

Thinking about running around in a bathing suit made me nervous. Possibly more nervous than fighting off looters in a blackout.

"We'd probably be safer at Marley's anyway," I said. "Marley could fight people off with his hockey sticks. Like, he's been saving for this his whole life."

"Marley would be useless in a crisis," said Desmond sharply.

"What's he gonna do, chug beer his way out of it?"

"Shut up," I said, but still smiling. "What would you do? Weed your way out of it?"

Desmond was very quiet during the rest of the twenty-five-minute walk to Marley's. I sank into thoughtfulness, too. Normally in summertime we were generally in a more carefree mood. Now that I think about it, it was the first summer of our conscious lives that Desmond and I didn't know what we were doing in September. Without the constant tiny goals of high school — end of class, end of day, exams, assignments — the future felt empty, scary and exhausting, like a cross-country bus trip.

Marley's house was on a side street in Kensington Market. The market itself was really just tenements held together with rat poo among small vintage and cheese stores at the base of Toronto Western Hospital. For some reason Toronto Western Hospital, which was a seven-story tall, beige brick building, had a huge smokestack. There was always sluggish grey smoke leaking from it. I felt like the smoke was from the burning of tumours and appendixes and amputated limbs and things. The little parkette across from Marley's house was covered in street kids from Quebec, who somehow managed to be both stylish and homeless at the same time.

I knew that once you got inside Marley's house, it looked like a magazine. His parents were successful web designers from back in the day. Before you could design your own web page, you had to hire people who did it for you for tens of thousands of dollars. Marley's parents got rich on that.

As we got closer, the sound of Marley's bass-heavy electronic music got louder. We rang the bell.

"Ayyyyy!" Marley opened the door. He hugged me and Desmond.

I crawled over bodies on the sectional — "Hey" "Hey" — to curl into the inside corner and sip my water bottle of gin.

We could have been an EDM music video. Lying over each other, lit by candles, the girls in their thin sleeveless tops and loose short shorts, the boys fully covered in long boardshorts and oversize T-shirts. It looked like in our culture, boys had to cover themselves, not girls.

Marley landed heavily beside me and stroked my hair a bit. "I love you, terrorist," he said.

He was on oxy and beer. He loved everyone. I let him run his wide Marley hand down to my shoulder and hook one of his meaty fingers into my bra strap, like I was a dog and he was gently hanging on to my collar in the park before he let me run. It was nice, but I had to be careful with Marley. He could start out all sweet and then — *boom!* — would get annoying.

Vivian popped into the room and everyone cheered. I clambered up off the couch and gave her a hug. In her high-cut jean shorts and a tube top she looked like one of those American Apparel ads pretending not to be pedophilia. But she was so confident she could get away with it. Her eyes were a bit glazed. Vivian did not have hang-ups about trying drugs. She called it research. I could tell she was on something, ecstasy probably, because she threw back her head and laughed hysterically at everything everyone said to her, even "Hi."

"What are you on?" I asked.

"Mushrooms," she whispered. "Don't you love everyone tonight? It's like the blackout has brought us all together."

We all hung out, listening to music and dancing for a couple of hours. Vivian seemed okay, but she was hugging and kissing everyone a bit more than usual. At one point, I saw her go straight up to Desmond, who was standing by the couch, put her hands behind his neck and tongue-kiss him. What? He sort of froze, eyes rolling, trying to be funny. But after a second he closed his eyes and kissed her back. Hey.

"Hey, Viv, what the hell ya doin'?" I yelled, and was immediately embarrassed. My heart stopped beating and was replaced by an empty balloon. Hmm, gin makes me aggressive, apparently.

Viv swayed away from Desmond, one hand still on his neck. "It's okay, honey," she said with a stupid smile.

My balloon stomach dropped and I saw Vivian suddenly as an empty Insta-addicted shallow girl. Or that's who she was when she was drinking or doing drugs. She was there but she was not there. Like a zombie. This is why I hated the drug scene. I always had. Vivian had always teased me that I was such a nice little Arab girl. A prude. Well, this prude had to stop herself from slapping her best friend in the face in a fit of jealousy. Suddenly I started to feel nauseous. I had to get out.

Desmond met my eye and raised his eyebrows. But his face was immediately dragged onto Viv's again, who was twisting his cheeks like plasticine in her fingers. Gross.

"Yeah," said Marley, and grabbed my face.

I jerked away. I am not into zombies.

I got up and went to Marley's kitchen before I left. They had a lot of cans of tuna in the pantry. The good kind. I put four cans into my backpack. I left. Turns out you can leave so easy with this crowd.

Survival Tip #11

Ten Uses for a Kaffiyeh

- Face mask
- Sling
- Tourniquet
- Fire starter
- Strainer

- Wrist brace
- Net
- Lamp wick
- Sack
- Trail marker

(The kaffiyeh is a brilliant survival tool. Originally a black-and-white-checkered headcloth that only men wore, it's now a combo of fashion statement and symbol of Palestinian support. Each of us have one of our own, ordered from the Palestinian factory Hirbawi in Hebron, to make sure we didn't get a made in China one.)

CHAPTER 11
The Encampment

I walked along College Street back towards home, alone. It was slightly cooler now that it was dark out, but still hot. I was disgusted with Vivian and still a bit drunk from the water-bottle gin. Oh, my God, alcohol was awful! Why do people drink it so much?

I passed by a convenience store lit by candles. Boy, it sure would be easy to steal canned goods and lighters from them. I walked by people eating ice cream on the stone steps of a church and then by those small grey men outside the coffee houses. The streetcars that usually clattered up and down College Street looked like huge exhausted animals who had sunk to their knees.

I got a text.

Desmond: *Hey, where are you?*

Desmond: *You ok?*

Desmond: *I left. Going home. Come to my house.*

Hah. I was mad. I ignored it.

Well, at least he left, too, and wanted to see me. So he and Vivian weren't a thing, I guess. I wasn't ready to forgive him yet, though. The memory of beautiful Viv with her cut-off shorts kissing him, and that second his eyes closed, really bugged me. I got mad all over again and decided to walk through the park to get home. It looked busy. There were little firepits, and flashlight beams pierced the dark tree foliage. The stars overhead looked like I had never

81

seen them before, almost smothering the sky with a blanket of white dots. There were about twelve people near the restroom area, where the weirdo guys usually hung out with their beards and scooters. I squinted. The weirdo guys were talking to mostly young people who were setting up tents. I could see the pale flutter of signs and banners, but couldn't read what they said.

A black dog ran up to me, barking.

"Hey, boy," I said, and patted his soft, round forehead.

"Douglas, *come here*! Sorry."

A woman ran up to me and grabbed the dog's collar. Hey! It was the climate change activist from the TV when I was watching with my Dad. She was wearing jeans and sandals, and her long brown hair was twisted with feathers now instead of being up in a bandana.

"Sorry about that," she said. "She loves people. She's totally safe."

"What's going on here?" I asked. "Some kind of festival?"

Normally I wouldn't ask such a direct question of strangers, but I was a bit uninhibited by the gin.

"It's an encampment to protest the government's lack of action against climate change," she said. "We were at Queen's Park and got kicked out, so we moved here. You are welcome to join us. I'm Jenny. We have activities and speeches planned all day tomorrow."

"Oh, wow," I said. "I'm totally into climate change."

"You are?" She looked quizzical.

Oh, no, it sounded like I was *for* climate change! How embarrassing!

A young man with long brown hair in a bun stumbled up to us. He was shirtless and he seemed out of it.

"Hey, Jenny," he said. "Where's the sleeping bags?"

"I think they're still in the U-Haul, Kyle," she said.

"Hey," Kyle said to me. "What's your name? Come here to support the protest?"

"No," I stammered. "I'm Jamilah. I mean, I'm, like, trying to prepare personally, though."

"Ahhh, you going to the march in Ottawa?" he asked.

"Yeah," I said. "But sometimes I wonder, like, what's the use? The government doesn't even listen."

Kyle nodded wildly.

"Let alone the corporations," added Jenny. "But there has been some change. There's the Paris Accord. We stopped a pipeline. We got Canada to reduce their emissions."

"Really?" I said. "I mean, is that going to make a difference if we're all out of power for months and fighting for water?"

I gestured at the scene around me. I wobbled a bit.

"No. I'm also taking care of myself." I leaned in confidentially. "I'm turning our garage into an off-the-grid bunker."

"Exactly, man!" said Kyle. "Anarchy. A survivalist!"

Jenny smiled at Kyle.

"Hey, Kyle, can you take Douglas with you to the field house?" She gestured at the dog. "She needs her dinner."

"Okay," Kyle said. "C'mon, Douglas!"

The dog followed him eagerly.

Jenny turned to me. "Kyle is cool," she said. "He's a psychiatric survivor."

"Oh," I said, not understanding. Man, was I ignorant.

"I think what we do will make a difference!" exclaimed Jenny. "If we don't stand up to the capitalist corporate greed, there will be no planet left."

"I guess," I said.

"I know it's scary," she said. "But if we all pull together, I believe we can make real change. Look." She rummaged through her multicoloured shoulder bag and pulled out a flyer. "That's tomorrow's schedule. We have speakers and sign-making and demonstrations."

I took it and absently took a sip from my gin water bottle.

"One thing," Jenny said eyeing the water bottle. "No alcohol in the encampment."

"Oh!" I said. "Right, I don't normally . . ." I heard my phone ping again. I hoped it was Desmond. "I, um. Okay. Um, I better go," I stammered, backing away. "Bye!"

Jenny waved. "Come back tomorrow and you can help us make some signs!" she called.

I checked my phone.

Desmond: *You ok? That was a stupid scene. Sleep tight.*

Poor Desmond. He was probably feeling the dumb gin, too. It was II p.m. Dad was going to kill me. But I *did* suddenly want to see Desmond. Everything felt scary or weird. The blackout, the party, the park. Mom and Dad never made me feel better. I felt like they only talked in clichés. But Desmond got me. Desmond made me feel safe. I dumped the water bottle in a trash can when I got to Bloor and headed up his street.

Me: *Coming*

Survival Tip #12

How to Survive a Coyote Attack

- Coyotes typically are wary of humans, but when coyotes band together to form packs, they can become quite dangerous, especially to pets and children.

- If you're walking a smaller dog, pick it up. For larger dogs, pull them in close to you. Always maintain control of your pet.

- Make yourself appear the bigger threat. Stand tall, stare into the eyes of the coyote and shout at it. You also can throw something at it. Do not run or turn your back. Running may change the coyote's assessment of you from aggressor to prey.

  (Once I was in High Park in the middle of the day and a coyote was resting in a field. Just like that. Lately there have been posters of lost small dogs — "Have you seen Fifi?" — with little mug shots of their silly faces. You are not supposed to let cats out of your house because they eat the birds, but also because the coyotes will eat the cats.)

CHAPTER 12
Under the Stars We Can Finally See

The side door leading to Desmond's basement was unlocked. I walked in quietly and headed down the stairs.

"Hey."

Desmond was coming up the stairs, wiping his hands on a cloth.

He stopped.

"I was cleaning," he said.

He was in jeans and a T-shirt, not shorts, and his shoulders didn't have their usual hunch. His eyes flicked up and down me. Was he *checking me out*?! I was used to other guys doing that. It was just an annoyance. When Desmond did it, it felt sweet. A bit alarming, but sweet.

"C'mon," he said, and led me downstairs. Even by the candlelight I could see he had cleaned up.

We sat on the couch and he looked at me. "I didn't want her to do that," he said.

"You," I said, "are not stoned."

He leaned back and half smiled. He was getting lines around his mouth and his jaw was looking harder. But his eyes were still mild. I leaned towards him and he went very still, watching me, his smile disappearing. His hand went behind my back and pulled me in closer. He looked me in the face. He was saying that it was up to me.

I kissed him. I didn't expect how he kissed me back, not like Marley. But I got more into it as his hand went to the back of my neck. I slumped into him.

"Let's go to your room," I said.

"Really?" He was serious. "Won't you get, like, disowned?"

We made out for a while. Both of us knew we weren't going to have sex, so it was normal and nice. Then we lay on our backs, and he pulled my hand to his chest, rubbing my thumb. He smiled goofily and I saw the eight-year-old boy I had first met. That might be a problem.

"Look," he said. "I found a portable generator that could work for the bunker."

He held up his phone and showed me the Canadian Tire site. It was the portable one with solar panels and the wind port.

"You are a man after my own heart," I said.

"I'm after more than that!" he goofed. He sat up and wiggled his eyebrows wildly to look like a cartoon pervert.

"Stop!" I said, laughing.

He lay back down. "I can't wait to go to the march," he said. "I'm looking at Airbnbs or something or a motel."

"Oh," I said, suddenly realizing how weird it would be to spend the night alone together on the road. "Maybe we can stay at my great-aunt Janice's. We can walk to Parliament Hill from there."

He made a face and reached for his pot vape. Ugh. Suddenly all my good feelings went away.

"I gotta go," I said.

"Oh." He looked disappointed. "I thought maybe we could hang."

"No, my dad will kill me."

"Okay, I'll walk you home."

We walked through the midnight dark streets under the stars

we could finally see. It still hadn't cooled off. When we got to my house, he kissed me.

"I'll call you later," I said as he walked away, a smile on his face.

Dad was up.

Survival Tip #13

How to Survive an Earthquake

- **Practise DROP, COVER and HOLD ON with all members of your household.**

  (No one will do it with me.)

- **During the earthquake, get under a table or desk. Hold on until shaking stops.**

- **Pick safe places in each room of your home. Contrary to popular belief, it is not safer in a doorway.**

- **Create an emergency survival kit that provides you and your pets with three days of non-perishable food and water, medicines, emergency radio and first aid materials. Keep in a reachable place.**

  (On it.)

- **Establish an out-of-the-area friend or contact that family members can check in with.**

  (We have earthquakes in Toronto. It's true. Not very often, but with fracking going on around the world, it's only going to get worse.)

CHAPTER 13
This Is Not Free

As soon as I walked up the path, I started to feel anxious and guilty. Hopefully I could go straight to bed and forget the whole stealing of the gin thing. But when I walked in the front door, I saw Dad waiting on the couch by a battery-operated lantern.

"My phone died." It wasn't true. I still had twenty per cent.

"You know you had to be home by ten," he said. "You know with this blackout the streets can be dangerous. Here you are always afraid, always talking about the danger, and you go out late on a dangerous night where there are hooligans."

"I was safe! I was with Desmond!" I exclaimed. Thank God he didn't know what Vivian's party was like.

"I know you were with Desmond," he said. "I saw the kissing in the street! You're kissing boys on the street?"

Oh, boy. I couldn't believe it. This was so frustrating. Everybody making fun of me for being a "good girl," and the one time — the one time! — I act like a normal teenager — *bam!* — he comes down on me like I'm a slut. I started to feel anger well up in me.

"I mean, it's just Desmond," I said lamely.

"Desmond is a good kid but I know he uses pot," said Dad. "This can make him crazy. Are you smoking this pot?"

"No!" I said. God, I hope he didn't know I vaped. If he saw my vape, he'd be sure I was smoking pot.

"I saw the gin bottle on the table," Dad continued. "What do you want to be? This drinking and trashing girl?"

"I just tasted it," I lied, glad I had thrown out the water bottle. "I am not trash."

"Jamilah, you know what happens to girls who drink and go out and see boys."

"What?" I was getting really angry. Maybe I wasn't a prude. So what if I wasn't?

"They get in trouble. And they deserve it!" he said. But I could tell he only half believed it. Still, it felt like a punch in the gut him saying that. Like he wanted me to be hurt.

"I don't deserve to get in trouble!"

"The boys they can't help themselves." He was trying to sound reasonable. "It becomes your fault."

Dad instantly looked like he regretted saying it, when he saw my mouth drop.

"Desmond is not like that," I said. (Although I guiltily admitted to myself that Marley was.) "Besides, you have this old-fashioned idea of girls. Maybe it's your stupid old-fashioned culture. You have to get over it, Dad."

Dad dropped his eyes. That was a mean thing to say to someone whose culture was disappearing, I realized. But I was so sick of being judged all the time as a girl. I was so sick of how we all had to be. Noor had it right, just abdicating from the heteronormative shit.

"Oh, Dad, I'm sorry . . ." I started. I was still angry, but now I was also sick with remorse.

"No!" thundered Dad. "This is why even more you have to go to university! Do you want to be a waitress or a cleaner for the rest of your life?"

"I don't know what to do anyway," I admitted. "I like science and building things, but my math was always too terrible."

"You can get a BA," he said. "Or you can work for the government." His tone softened. "You're a person that needs stability, Jamilah."

"Why don't you give Noor a hard time?" I said. "She's always with Beth."

"Noor does not have this anxiety," said Dad. "She does not have this nervousness you have. She has good marks. She can be a good pharmacist."

"Or a doctor," I said. "You know, like George. Just 'cause she's a girl doesn't mean she can't be a doctor. All you say for her is pharmacist. And George a doctor."

"She is more responsible than you," said Dad, ignoring my comments. "She doesn't run around with boys."

"She's a lesbian *witch*," I shrieked.

He tsked. "This is just child's play." He stood up. "Enough. If you are not going to university, you are not getting a job, you come home late and drinking, then you are not contributing to this family!"

"I am doing something useful!" I insisted. "When I finish the garage, you will see I am the only one thinking! I am trying to make us safe."

"Safe! You are safe!" he said. "If you knew what we went through back home. Are you kidding with this nervousness? A bomb landed on the buildings across our street in Haifa. It was Hamas, but they apologized. When Israel wants to cut off water or take water from Gaza or cousin Moussa in Bethlehem, they cut off the power. In Gaza, we are in a wall and they bomb us, we cannot escape. You are free here. You are a stupid, spoiled girl!"

"This is not free!" I screamed and stormed up to my room. I was stung he had called me stupid, and I was tired of getting compared to Noor. I spied Mom's wallet on the table by the stairs. That's it. I slipped out her credit card. I was going to order that generator. I was going to build the safe house and they would see. I threw myself on my stupidly hot bed and went to my phone. There it was. So beautiful. "The Natural solar and wind-powered generator, $1,899."

I stared at it, my heart thumping. It's true, I was a total loser. I couldn't do anything right. My clothes were always messed up, I was being a baby with my eco-anxiety and I wasn't going to university. My throat felt like it was closing and tears came to my eyes as I realized what a joke I was and how useless I was. To my family and to my friends. Except Desmond.

I looked at the generator.

"The best portable power and uses free energy from the sun. Can power refrigerators, electronics and power tools."

They wouldn't be making fun of me if we had it now, humming away.

I ordered it, holding my breath as I typed in Mom's credit card. I chose two-day delivery for extra and collapsed on my pillow, covered in sticky sweat, dehydrated and already hungover. I got up again and ran a T-shirt under cold water in the bathroom, took off my dress and put the T-shirt on. I crawled back into my bed and lay there, temporarily damp and cool, certain I wouldn't fall asleep. But I did. I was exhausted from the walking and the heat and the fight with my dad. And deep down I felt sick I had insulted him. But why couldn't he see? I think I could still taste the awful gin in my mouth. I fell asleep to the whoops of the blackout parties and the distant scraping of the skateboards.

Survival Tip #14

How to Survive a Flood

- **Move immediately to higher ground.**

    (Hmm, I was going to have to build a deck on the garage.)

- **Move important indoor items to the highest floor.**

- **Unplug appliances.**

- **Avoid walking or driving through flood waters.**

- **Stock your emergency preparedness kit.**

    (Hello!)

CHAPTER 14
In Search Of

The next morning was still a blackout and still really hot. My phone was dead. I plugged it into the battery pack. Immediately, a text from Vivian popped up.

Vivian: *Hey you mad?*

Vivian: *I'm sorry. Can I make it up to you?*

Vivian: *I was just crazy on Molly.*

Mad? I don't know if I was mad anymore. Desmond and I were good now. Real good. Actually I felt a little embarrassed for her.

Me: *I'm not mad.*

Me: *Anymore.*

Vivian: ♥ ♥

I avoided Dad and walked out to the backyard where Teta was calmly making coffee over the firepit as if she had never had electricity. She handed some me rosewater shortbread and a tiny cup of coffee. I stood and looked at the bicycles on the ground by the garage.

"Why you make this garage?" Teta asked me, lifting the tiny coffee pot off the flame as it frothed over.

"If there's a disaster, we are safe. It's a safe place to hide."

Teta sighed and shrugged. "Is safe here," she said. "Back home no home. Everybody bombs."

I walked over and leaned against my Teta's broad side.

There was no conflict in any way leaning on her. It was like pure love. Love in a polyester housedress.

"Very good girl," she said. "Very beautiful." She chuckled with real amusement. Real joy. As if we were safe. "Boy for you?"

"Ugh. *La*, Teta, *la*," I said, telling her no.

"Is okay, *habibti*." She took a deep breath. "Is better you are free."

Noor came downstairs and up to us. She was wearing a tank top and had turned her kaffiyeh into a sarong skirt.

Teta's eyes widened. "Ah, no! This is for your head!" she exclaimed. "Sido would say this is not proper. *Non, non, habibti*."

"But doesn't it look nice?" Noor dramatically twirled and posed in front of Teta.

Teta laughed and gave Noor a kiss, rubbing her buzz-cut hair. "You need to wear on your head."

"I thought you didn't like the veil," said Noor.

"This time, for you I like. You can wear it like a boy."

We all laughed.

"Boy for you?" she asked Noor.

"I am the boy for me," said Noor.

Teta narrowed her eyes and wagged her finger at Noor, but her eyes twinkled and she went back to making coffee. She had married Sido at fifteen, and things had been a lot stricter then. He had been a young civil servant in Palestine under the British and he was very strict about doing things correctly. When Israel was founded in 1948, he was shocked to find himself a second-class citizen. He was at least as good as the beloved British. And better educated and more proper than most. He complained all the time we didn't dress formally enough when he got to Canada. Teta loved him deeply, but since losing him five years ago, I think she was, at eighty-seven, becoming a rebel!

Noor fixed her glance on me. "So," she whispered, when Teta went to wash her hands. "You and Desmond are an item?"

"OMG. You saw us kiss, too?"

"Boy, was Dad mad when he saw the gin out."

"Ssssh," I said, pointing to Teta. "Yeah, it was intense. C'mon, look at the stuff I found in the garage."

Noor and I walked over to the pile of accumulating junk.

"You know," she said. "You could sell this stuff on Marketplace or trade this stuff on Bunz."

"Bunz?"

"The Trading Zone. It's a 'buy nothing' site. It's good for the environment," she explained. "Here."

She pulled out her phone and we plopped down beside each other on the grass.

It was a lot of clothes. Most of the girls' clothes on Bunz were tiny tank tops or twisted shorts pressed flat on a floor or a bed. I couldn't figure out why they seemed so familiar till I realized that most TV crime procedurals and HBO and Netflix shows had some version of those images. I was really getting tired of the murdered girl thing, and now I couldn't even scroll though Bunz without feeling nervous at a picture of girls' clothes.

I downloaded Bunz on my own phone and scrolled through the day's posts: half-empty bottles of olive oil or booze. Ugh. And who would trade for an opened box of crackers on Bunz? There was a section just for succulents, those tiny cactuses Noor was obsessed with. They were pretty cute, all green and sturdy and miniature. The interface was a great design. It looked happy, with a blog and everything. What was ISO? Oh "in search of." Okay, what was I in search of? Stuff to stock the bunker.

I typed in "solar." I got:

Solar flashlight:

"A solar-powered flashlight that has just won multiple awards. Just place the flashlight in the light and the built-in solar cells will

99

charge the rechargeable batteries. Perfect for emergencies. Makes a great gift for Dad."

Why not a mom? The value was listed as twenty dollars.

I looked at the ISO of the post. Dude's ISO included tequila, men's chunky jewelry and cigarette cases. His photo was a blurry close-up of a man's face with a black goatee. I realized I was going to have to come up with things to trade. I wondered if Desmond had any men's chunky jewelry.

"Noor, look at this guy." I held up my phone to her.

She stopped and peered into it.

"His ISO is like a douchebag to-do list," I said.

We scrolled through more of the offerings. Old books. Coats. Half-empty cereal boxes.

"Who would want a half-empty cereal box? It could have rat poison in it," said Noor.

"Someone who really loves cereal and is really, really poor," I replied.

"Someone whose mom is like, 'I buy the groceries and in this house we eat Shredded Wheat not Cap'n Crunch,'" laughed Noor.

"'I'll show you, Mom,'" I said in a voice I thought such a loser would sound like.

"I have a profile," said Noor.

Noor's little profile photo was a close-up of a mandala and her ISO was plants, candles ("unscented soy") and anything "Wiccan."

"Let's set you up," she said. "What do you want?"

Well, I knew I didn't need a generator anymore. "Solar-powered stuff, batteries, LÄRABARs, candles, lighters," I said.

"Okay, what do you have to post?"

"I don't know! Maybe some old clothes."

"You must have lots of old clothes," she said. "You've been at least three different sizes in the past year and all you wear now is bike shorts and T-shirts."

"Bitch," I said.

"No, you look good now!" she said. "The best. C'mon, let's go look in your room."

"Agh. It is so hot in there," I said.

"You'll get used to it."

We went to my room and Noor opened my closet door.

"Wait!" I called out but it was too late.

"What the *eff*?" she exclaimed.

She was looking at my stash of canned goods and stuff. She flipped open a shoebox that said "AA batteries" on the outside.

"Is this why we never have batteries?" she asked.

"I buy them, too," I said defensively.

She looked back in the closet then looked at me steadily for a second.

"Tuna?"

I shrugged.

"Where're your clothes?"

"Under the bed in bins."

We pulled out the two bins. They were crammed with my old smaller jeans, summer dresses and sweaters. We sat on the bed and scrolled on the app to get more ideas. There were a lot of small, dark-haired girls with anime expressions on their faces looking limply into the camera. Even though one of them was only modelling a jean jacket, she still looked like she was for sale. I felt uneasy. Did I want to be this exposed? I realized our bodies were everywhere now because of Insta and pornography. Everywhere in a way that they weren't before. A few girls were even modelling disposable club wear, looking very seventies porno with their splotchy leg skin. Don't look as good without our Insta filter, do we?

"Look, no matter what you do, you look like you're for sale," I observed. "Do all girls on any screen become automatic porn?"

"Yeah," said Noor. "If you're a predatory douche."

"You have to assume the 'predouche' is everywhere," I said, smiling.

"Beware of the Predouche!" crowed Noor, her hands in the air.

We giggled. Noor and I didn't always get along like this. She hadn't used her Wise Woman voice once. I was happy. It reminded me of times when we were little, playing with our toys together.

"We invented a word!" I said. "Okay, we'll just take pictures of the clothes on the floor."

"Hey, remember when the *Weekly Magazine* had all the people for sale in the back?" asked Noor.

The free *Weekly Magazine* used to have full-colour sex worker ads in the back pages. They said they did it to be inclusive, but the side effect was that all over the city people had to look at women's bodies for sale, since the magazines were lying all over the subway and restaurant tables. So even kids had to see it. Take it from me, it does not make a little girl feel good to know how easily she can be sold or rented.

"Remember when Mom painted the front hall and there was newspaper on the floor covered with the naked women's bodies for, like, a week?" asked Noor.

"Yeah, and some dudes," I said. "At least the dudes were cute."

Mom hadn't even noticed she had used the sex worker pages. She was probably meditating while she worked. The baseboards were half done, which was Mom's way. She gets to things eventually (although none of our curtains had hems), so all the tits and bums and blank eyes were still lying on the floor, begging for attention we all knew they didn't really want. I guess we just stopped seeing them until one day when Teta had the priest and the church ladies over for coffee and cake. The ladies had giggled and the priest had just looked shocked.

We lay my clothes on the floor and took the pictures.

"Okay," said Noor. "What else do you have to offer?"

"I dunno," I said. "I can trade stuff in the garage. Want to help me clear it out?"

"Uh, no," she said. "I got to go to work. If they need me."

She got up, started backing out of my room.

"Don't forget to put *tuna* and *batteries* in your ISO!" she taunted, and bolted away.

I threw a shoe after her. She screamed and was gone.

I needed Desmond. I texted him.

Me: *Come over need help emptying garage and Bunz buddy.*

Desmond: *Bunz buddy huh didn't think you were into that.*

Me: *Ew*

Dot dot dot.

Desmond: *Kidding! sure, I'll help.*

I worked on my ISO.

- batteries
- solar stuff
- protein bars
- saw
- rugs
- a stovetop kettle (that was for the family in general)

I went downstairs and out the back door. It was time to face the music with Dad. There he was, charring eggplants to make the baba ghanouj. He chars hundreds of them every year, then peels them and puts their guts in freezer bags so we always have yummy, roasty-tasting baba in the winter. My heart clenched as I looked at him, so meek and attentive to the eggplants, his short-sleeved plaid shirt already sweat-stained under the arms. And here I was making his life worse.

"Dad, I'm sorry," I said. "I'll get a job. I will."

"*Habibti*," he said. "I only want you to be safe, too."

"I know," I said. "But look, I can make us money selling the garage stuff." I was guiltily thinking about paying off the generator. "And it's really a science experiment, right? It's like a course. I'm not doing nothing."

"All right, we'll see," he said. "But no drinking, you understand?"

"Of course! No! I hate it, yeah!" I fervently agreed. That would be easy.

"Don't throw out the secateurs," he added without looking up from the grill. Good. We were okay.

I opened the garage side door. It popped open with its usual moist squeak. The garage was starting to look almost like you could live in it. I decided to post the elliptical on Marketplace, but thought the exercise bike could be updated to an energy converter, so I kept it. Can you turn an exercise bike into a generator? If only there was a way to connect gyms to power grids! I started arranging things to take pictures of them.

"Hey."

I turned. It was Desmond. I wasn't sure if we should kiss.

"Hey," I said, and caught a glimpse of myself in the old dresser mirror. Oh. My. God. My bedhead was insane, flat on one side and frizzy on the other. I pulled a hair elastic off my wrist and did the thing where you spread it out like a fan on top.

"Hmm, very bold fashion statement," said Desmond, then looked around. "Okay, what have we got here?"

I knew better than to interrupt him when he stood there zoned out with focus. He clocked every wall, stared at the dresser in the middle and then looked at me.

"We need a garbage section and a keep section and a things-to-repair section," he said decisively.

"And a Bunz section," I said. "Did you say hi to my dad? Was he weird?"

"What? You told him?" Desmond looked terrified.

"Well, he figured it out when he saw you drop me off last night," I said. "He was up."

"Oooh, God," moaned Desmond, remembering last night. "No, I said 'Hey, Mr. Mansour' and he just grunted."

Oh, good. Just grunting *was* normal. Dad had never learned the smiley smiley Western culture niceties.

We started on the garage. It was filthy work. First, we carried everything we could outside to the alley, stacking the garbage against one wall. Mom brought us lemonade and I sat with her at the picnic table watching Desmond work on the bicycles. He looked pretty cute, squatting beside the pedals and trying to make a wheel straighter.

Mom came up to us and watched for a minute as I put ashtrays in the donate box.

"Oh, my God, I'm so embarrassed about those ashtrays," she said. "I quit when I got pregnant with you."

We smiled at each other.

"You know that's why I want you to stop vaping," she said.

My smile dropped. "Mom! I will!" Agh! She was always on me.

"Sit down," she said.

We sat in the lawn chairs. Desmond stayed by a bike, fiddling with it.

"Your father and I were talking . . ." she said.

Dad had gone inside.

"Desmond, this is about you, too."

Desmond put a wrench down and slowly stood up.

"You know we don't like you driving to Ottawa together. And staying overnight in Ottawa," said Mom.

"Oh, my God, Mom!" I said. I was immediately embarrassed, picturing Mom picturing me and Desmond in a hotel.

"And we are not happy you are not going to university this year."

"There's no point," I said. "Universities are just money-grabbing corporate entities contributing to the problem."

"Jamilah, don't start," warned Mom. "But we are impressed with your commitment to this off-the-grid project. We have decided that, if you get a job this year, we will let you take next year off school. But you must get a job."

"Really?"

"And I have good news," she continued. "Mrs. Vogel wants to talk to you. Her company has a government-funded training program available for girls who want to get more into STEM. She would like to know if you are interested in applying. It's for researching homes in the area that could be adapted to solar."

"Really?" I asked. "She'll take me?"

"But I want to say again. We don't want you going with Desmond alone to the march."

I groaned. This was both embarrassing (like, are my parents picturing me having sex all the time?) and inconvenient.

She smiled. "You may drive up with Desmond, but you are taking George with you in the car," she said. "You will stay with my aunt Janice and uncle Phil."

I looked at Desmond's face. It was extremely expressionless, so I could tell he was disappointed. Was I feeling a little relieved? I was. I guess I'll never stop being the prude. But to be honest, we have always loved visiting Mom's aunt Janice and uncle Philip. They lived in a great neighbourhood and they had a pool.

Mom slapped her hands on her knees lightly, stood up, then bent down to gently grab my chin and tilt my head to her. I was so surprised I didn't even flick her off.

"I repeat," she said, looking me straight in the eye. "I'll give you a year. Then you're going to university."

Survival Tip #15

How to Disappear

(According to a doomsday prepper online, here are some tips on disappearing.)

- **First of all, start distancing yourself from others. You have to come up with excuses constantly to not hang with people until the lies become your new reality.**
  (Wait, that's Noor.)

- **Start withdrawing all your money.**
  (Hah.)

- **Quit your job.**
  (Hah.)

- **Kill your social media accounts.**
  (That would be a big heads-up, though. This guy is old.)

- **Destroy your pictures and avoid new ones.**
  (Again, impossible in this day and age.)

- **Change up your appearance, dye your hair and wear a hat.**
  (What is this, a cartoon?)

- **Practise new mannerisms.**
  (An accent?)

- **Destroy your phone.**

CHAPTER 15
No Phones in the Apocalypse

We got a lot done on the garage. A new dad came by after seeing a posting and bought the elliptical for sixty dollars. He said his wife had just had a baby and wanted to get back in shape. Dad said I could keep the money. I felt guilty for a second about the generator, but decided I would put the money towards that.

"*Habibti*," called up Teta the next morning. "Community centre has power."

Oh, shoot, I was supposed to go help the Syrians today. I guiltily took out my vape and took a few hits, knowing I couldn't do it around the kids. I looked at the evil cylinder. I had to stop this. Okay, this was the last cartridge. Why doesn't George help the kids anyway? I'd been babysitting from the age of thirteen.

I joined Teta downstairs and we walked down to the community centre. When we came to the park, she was alarmed by the brightly crowded tents and flags. It did look kinda dirty.

"*Haram*," she said, which she uses as "Oh, no." "What is this?"

"Just a demonstration," I said. "We can go through it. They are nice."

"*La! La!*" said Teta. She refused to walk through the park and we went down the side street instead, crossing the street when she saw the police car parked on the road.

"*Assalamu alaykum*," said Asma when we walked into the

basement community kitchen. Malik was sitting in her lap, eating dry Cheerios.

"*Wa alaykuma assalam*," I said.

"Can you take five minutes?" Asma asked me. "We have prayer."

She handed me Malik, who squirmed, then went with the other women to a corner of the room and faced east and started to pray. Teta looked at me.

"These are very good ladies," she said.

She pulled out her rosary.

"Go take this boy outside," she commanded me.

Malik was in a tiny three-piece suit. Probably a donation from the Portuguese OGs (Original Grannies) from one of their endless weddings. I noticed a lot of the newcomer kids are often dressed as fancy as possible. Especially since 9/11, we Arabs always have to prove we aren't savages to the Westerners. I know because I have old Arabic relatives who don't so much get judgmental as frightened when I show up at events or at church in, like, even jeans. That day I was careful to be wearing mom jeans (literally my mom's) and a white T-shirt so I wouldn't offend anybody with my boobs or legs or bike shorts. They do *not* get bike shorts.

I took little Malik's hand and walked him out back. The only outside access was through the kitchen to the garbage cans. It wasn't pretty out there, but everything was fascinating to Malik: the milk crates with plastic ashtrays on them, the pavement crack dandelions and even the chain-link fence between the community centre property and the house next door with a truck in the driveway. Malik immediately picked a dandelion and held it up to me proudly. A dark-haired young man came out of the house and got into the truck. He looked out the driver's side window at Malik, who rushed to the fence. With his soft little hands against the wire and the limp dandelion still drooping in one fist, he looked like a Red Cross optic.

"I have one that age," said the man, smiling.

Then he got in his truck and backed out. Malik called to him through the fence as he drove away. He must have reminded him of his father. Then he cried for his mother, so I carried him back inside. She was ready and took him.

"*Shukran*," she said, thanking me. "*Khalas, khalas*," she said to her son, cajoling him to stop crying and feeding him a cookie.

There was a whooping and some clattering and Leila and Aziz clambered into the room.

"Jamilah! Jamilah!"

"Can we fix our bikes?"

"*Shway, shway*," I said. "Calm down."

They laughed hysterically at my accent.

"*Shway, shway*," they mocked.

"Okay if they come to my house?" I asked Mona.

She nodded.

I don't know why, it may have been the promise of bicycles, but Leila and Aziz were positively dancing around me as we made our way back up the street. They were like different kids now that they knew me. Suddenly I had a thought. What if *I* was the safe place for them in this long journey they've been on? And if I can take care of them, maybe I could take care of myself, too?

"Get out of the road and stay on the sidewalk," I said in a stern voice to practise being in charge.

OMG. They took no offense and obeyed immediately! When we walked through the park, I saw Jenny and waved. There were several police officers there now, looking bored and hot and standing under the big trees. The kids grew silent and looked down, standing closer by my side. Leila even slipped her hand into mine. When we got to my house, they ran into the backyard via the alley like it was theirs. I followed, checking the hydro app. Yup, almost full power restored in the city of Toronto. Just a few dark spots in East York. But I knew this was not over. What if the power went out in winter?

Insulation. I was going to have to figure out insulation.

Lying on the ground were two kids' bikes. Both had flat tires and one was missing a seat. Mom's bike was also lying out, suffering from a combo of broken gears and flat tires. It hadn't been ridden in about five years. Desmond had started working on the bikes, so the toolbox was out.

I pointed to the kids' bikes.

"You know what?" I said. "If you fix them, you can have them."

"Really?!" said Aziz, and turned to his sister with a smile.

They crouched down to examine the bikes. I looked at them fondly. It was no longer a chore to babysit these guys. If anyone knew how to bloom where they were planted, it was them. I could use some of their courage and resourcefulness. I went on Bunz and added a children's bike seat to my ISO.

"So, what's your favourite food in Canada?" I asked the kids.

"Pizza," they both said.

"Mine's grape leaves," I said.

"You make grape leaves?" asked Aziz. "Like us in Syria?"

"Yup," I said. "Israel and Palestine are very close to Syria, so a lot of the food is the same. We get the leaves right off that vine Dad grows."

I waited a moment, then asked, "How was school when you got here?"

They went quiet.

"Okay," said Aziz finally, turning the bigger kids' bike upside down and rotating the pedals.

Leila grabbed a rag and started cleaning the other bike. Again I realized they were so capable compared to me. I thought of all the things they were going through, and yet how they still kept trying at things.

"The other children call us terrorists," said Leila. "I don't like my clothes. They are old from other children."

"Shut up, Leila," said Aziz.

"The other kids call Aziz Osama," continued Leila. "'Osama, hey, Osama,' when he plays football. But he is the best player. They like him. There is one bad boy. He says his father is a soldier and kills us."

"*Khalas*, Leila," said Aziz. "I don't care."

Leila ran up to me and whispered, "What is 'Sand . . .'" she uttered the n word.

Holy crap! My mouth went dry and I absently reached for my vape so I could think. Ooops, no! Not in front of the kids!

"We never say that word," I said. "That word means that boy has bad parents and wasn't taught right from wrong. It's a very bad word, especially against Black people and people of colour."

I didn't want to get more into it. It would freak her out if she thought some people thought she wasn't even human. I remember Vivian once told me that when she was eight her parents explained the Holocaust to her and she kept asking them, "But why do they hate us?" for, like, two years.

"I was too young," Vivian had said. "I felt sad for a while all the time."

I made a note to tell Mona she needed to explain more to them about the n word's history here. Or maybe Desmond. But wait, that would just bum him out. He's always having to explain racism and microaggressions.

"Jamilah!"

It was Dad.

"*Jamilah*, come here!"

Dad was out front. Now what? I scooted down the side of the house to the front where there was a delivery person standing next to a big box on a dolly. It was the generator. Dad was holding a paper in his hand.

"What is this?"

Oh, God. "Okay, don't get mad," I said. "I meant to tell you. I'll pay for it. I ordered it."

"You *ordered* it?!"

"Dad, we're going to need one!" I said. "You know that. I'll pay for it. I got the sixty dollars from Marketplace for the elliptical and there's more stuff. Mrs. Vogel offered me a summer job . . ."

"You ordered it? You ordered it with what?" He looked at the paper in his hand. "It says $2,200!"

He raised the paper and looked like he was going to swipe me across the face with it. "What did you pay for this with?"

"On a credit card."

"What credit card?"

"Uhm, I borrowed Mom's?"

"Your *mother's* card?"

"Sir, where would you like me to put this?" asked the delivery person.

"Put it back on the truck!" yelled Dad. "Take it back!"

"I'm sorry." The delivery person took a picture of it. "I can't take it back. If you want to return it, you have to contact the company."

"I will not sign," said Dad.

"Sir, you don't have to. We have the proof of delivery here." He held up his phone.

The delivery person expertly dipped the two heavy boxes off the dolly. One was tall and thin and probably held the solar panels, and the other was for the generator itself (well, it was half boxed with wheels showing underneath). He walked back to his truck and jumped in.

"I could make you be arrested for this," said Dad. "I should. I have had it with you. You are drinking and out late with a boy and you are obsessed with this climate disaster and you are not going to school and now you are a thief. A *thief*."

I put my head down. Tears started falling down my cheeks. "I just think you guys aren't paying attention!" I cried. "We're all going to die. Can't you see? I'm the only one preparing and you think it's more important for me to just be a good little girl. You want me to die from being a good little girl!"

"*You are a thief!*"

George ran out to the front porch and looked down. "What's that, man? Looks cool!" he said.

"*George, get back in the house!*" yelled Dad.

George looked stricken and darted back in.

"You act like you are not a member of this family!" Dad yelled at me.

"Fine, I'll leave!" I screamed.

Where would I go? I could stay at Vivian's, or Desmond's. Or wait! I could go to the encampment.

Noor walked up the front path, coming home from the coffee shop.

"What the hell is this?" she asked.

I turned to her. "Take care of the kids. They're in the backyard."

I ran up to my room to grab my go bag and ran outside again.

"You are not going to this trip to Ottawa!" Dad yelled after me.

I twisted past the boxes on our front path and ran down the street towards the park, my bag bouncing clumsily on my shoulder. Was I the only one who cared? Deep down, I knew it had been wrong of me to spend more than $2,000 on Mom's card. But I could justify it.

But was I turning wild and going crazy, living in this fear all the time? It was too much. My anxiety was too much. I was too much.

I reached for my vape in the outside pocket of the bag. Oh, no. No vape pen. And oh, no! No phone. They were on my bedside table. Oh, God. Now Mom was going to kill me when she found the vape pen. I laughed bitterly. Another nail in my coffin. Then I realized I hadn't vaped the whole time I was with the kids. Again. Maybe I didn't need it. Addictions are a liability for a survivalist, after all. I stopped running, straightened up and started walking purposefully. Hopefully the encampment would take me. I didn't even need my phone. There are no phones in the apocalypse. I was going to disappear.

Survival Tip #16

How to Be Arrested

(I found this on a site called PEN Canada. It's an organization that helps free writers who are imprisoned and persecuted around the world. They even have a T-shirt for protesting. It's black with yellow lettering.)

FRONT:

"I HAVE THE RIGHT TO DEMONSTRATE PEACEFULLY AND EXPRESS MY OPINION"

BACK:

"POLICE CANNOT:

ARREST ME FOR TAKING PHOTOS.

USE PHYSICAL FORCE UNLESS I AM ENGAGING IN ILLEGAL ACTIVITY.

FORCE ME TO DELETE DATA OR RECORDINGS OR TO REMOVE THIS SHIRT."

(I want one. Meanwhile, I'm supposed to write my lawyer's number on my arm when I protest. So I better get a lawyer.)

CHAPTER 16
Climate Rebellion

It was about noon and there were a lot more tents and people at the park. The tents were not just by the restroom building but extended towards the street under the trees. There was a U-Haul parked on the street by the park entrance. I looked around. The grass and the trees looked sort of dusty and crushed from heat. It felt more like an animal enclosure than a park. One of those really generous animal enclosures, for sure, but still an animal enclosure. Because you can't really forget the wide, busy road all along the west side, and the mall that lies across that street like a minimum-security prison.

Now I could read the banners. Hung along the park fence was a white sheet that said "CLIMATE JUSTICE REBELLION" and "CLIMATE JUSTICE IS RACIAL JUSTICE." The air was so heavy and still the banners didn't even ripple.

Jenny was there by the entrance, talking into what looked like a reporter's phone. When she was done, and the guy wearing a press badge walked away, she saw me and waved me over.

"Hi! How's it going?" she asked. "Gonna help us make some signs today?"

"Yeah," I said. "Um, I was actually wondering if I could camp out here."

Jenny narrowed her eyes.

"How old are you?"

"Eighteen," I lied.

"Did something happen?"

"Look, I live up the road. My parents are okay with this," I lied again. "They are actually bringing some food later."

"Oh, sure, then we have a couple extra tents." Jenny led me to a bright green tent set up near the playground. "You can have this one," she said.

It was pretty close to two others that already looked inhabited. One even had potted tomato plants in front of it.

"That's Carol's," said Jenny. "She takes those wherever she goes."

A long-limbed woman with curly grey hair crawled out of one of the tents. She was in cargo shorts and a T-shirt that read "PEN Canada." It said "If You Are Arrested" in big letters and listed in small print a bunch of details. I started to try to read it then realized I was staring at her chest.

"Hi," she said. "Welcome. You don't snore, do you?"

"No," I said. Oh, my God. What was I getting into?

"Well, he does," she said, jerking her thumb to the other tent.

Jenny looked disapproving. "C'mon, Carol," she said. "This is communal living! But, okay."

She turned to me. "He's what we like to call around here a 'tourist' at these events. His name is Terence." She giggled. "Terence the Tourist. He usually sleeps at his parents' and treats this like a vacation. And worse, he somehow always manages to get a girlfriend at these gatherings. We think he's here so he can drink in peace, but we haven't caught him yet."

"Take a corner," said Carol.

We all leaned down and unhooked a corner of the tent peg.

"Hey!" Up walked a twentyish guy with a shaggy head of blond hair and several small face tattoos. He was wearing black cut-off sweatpants and a black tee with the arms cut off. "Hey, ladies. Whatchya doin?" he asked.

"Dude, you snore," said Carol. "I'm moving my tent."

He looked all apologetic. "Shit, Carol, so sorry. I'll help you."

We all leaned down and grabbed a corner. He looked across the tent at me and winked. I literally had to fight looking behind me to see what he was winking at. It was like a wink from one of Mom's black-and-white movies. So *corny*! Who does that? Ew.

"Okay, let's go," said Jenny. "I'll show you where we eat. We all eat communally at the picnic tables by the field house. Do you need a bag and a pillow?"

"Oh, no! Yeah, I forgot," I blustered.

"Not to worry. Fortunately, the community is contributing," she said. "To be honest, we have, like, ten extra tents. Sometimes neighbours bring food or clothes or soap, or sometimes they just come and hang out. Let's get you a pillow!"

We walked past tents and firepits. We got to the U-Haul where a big guy with a close black beard was organizing stuff.

"Hey, man," he said when he saw Jenny. "I think we have enough canned food." He gestured at five crates of canned soup.

"Can we somehow tell them to stop? Nicely?" Jenny asked.

"I'll take it!" I said before I could stop myself.

The guy's expression didn't change but I knew I had made a faux pas. "We'll donate it to the foodbank," he said, smiling easily.

"Omar, can we get a bag and pillow for our friend, here?" asked Jenny.

"What's your name?" asked Omar.

"Jamilah."

"Jamilah? That's my sister's name! Where you from?"

"My dad's from Haifa." I felt a pang thinking of my dad. My dad who hates me right now. "Mom's from here."

"Ahh!" said Omar. "I'm from Bethlehem! I'm studying engineering here on a student visa. My name's Omar."

"*Marhaba.*"

"*Marhaba.*"

Jenny looked at me. "You're Indigenous?"

"No, half-Palestinian."

"You know, especially with the effects of climate change, many of us consider Palestinians an Indigenous people?" said Jenny. "You could be part of the Indigenous Climate Action group. And you have to meet Danielle. She runs a beautiful dance group that is working with kids from Canada and Palestine."

"Really?" I thought I could do that. Maybe all that folk dancing from my childhood wouldn't go to waste.

Kyle ran up. He reminded me of a puppy, his long hair bouncing. He was blinking rapidly, smiling and not smiling every few seconds. He seemed a bit hyper. "Jenny, Jenny, come on!" he panted. "The police are serving us a notice of trespass! Those pigs!"

"Don't worry," said Omar to me. "That happens all the time. C'mon, I'll walk you to your tent and show you around."

Omar showed me the field house. It was a brick building that had the washroom, which frankly smelled pretty bad in the heavy, dank air. It smelled like industrial-strength air freshener, piss and shit. I hope that smell couldn't reach my tent. I was thinking furiously about what Jenny had said. Palestinians Indigenous People? Huh. And if you really think it through, Jews are Indigenous people of that land, too. Vivian and I were cousins! Suddenly I missed Vivian. She would be so great to be with now. She'd let me vent about Dad and we'd be laughing at Terence the Tourist together. If I had my phone, I would text her.

We passed a young police officer slouching on a bench with his bike leaning against it. The hair under his helmet was dark with sweat and he was wearing a bulletproof vest over his shirt and heavy shorts.

"You okay, Officer?" asked Omar.

"Man, it's this heat," said the officer. "I can't deal with it."

I was surprised how young he looked. Not much older than me.

Omar pulled a water bottle from his bag and handed it to the officer. "You gotta hydrate, man," Omar said. "Reuse that bottle, though."

The young cop took it. "Thanks," he said. "I'm Officer Maclean." He took a swig. "Hey, listen," Officer Maclean said and stood up. I felt Omar tense a bit. "I'm gonna do you a favour. You guys can stay here. But you have to remove the extension cords and firepits. You're getting served a notice today."

"Right, okay." Omar relaxed.

We kept walking. I looked at him.

"You looked like you thought he was gonna arrest you or something when he stood up," I said.

"Yeah, growing up in the West Bank, you get to be pretty nervous around the police," he said. "From both sides."

Still, I felt a bit sorry for Officer Maclean in his bulletproof vest. I was feeling the heat, too. For a second I thought longingly of my window AC unit.

"I'll show you where we make some signs. You want to help?" asked Omar.

"Sure."

Several tables were lined up under a canopy tent and lots of poster board and paint were lying on the lawn. There were about six people working on the signs. A lady with dreads smiled at me and a young blonde girl in cut-offs handed me a poster board. She had her face painted blue and green and her hair was all chewed up with worn-out pink extensions.

She handed me a piece of paper. "Hi," she said. "I'm Justine. Here's a list of slogans if you want. You can do your own, too."

They were pretty funny.

"JUST LIKE ICE CAPS, I'M HAVING A MELTDOWN"

"FRACK OFF, GAS HOLES"

"IF YOU WERE SMARTER, I'D BE IN SCHOOL"

"WE ARE THE CHANGE AND CHANGE IS COMING!"

"IF NOT NOW, WHEN?"

Hah! "IF YOU WERE SMARTER, I'D BE IN SCHOOL." I liked that one! I happily worked on the signs for a few hours, moving from bit of shade to bit of shade under the unrelenting sun. Insects whined and poor Douglas was under a table panting heavily. But this was so much better than doomscrolling. I wondered if Dad had returned the generator yet. Better not to think about that. What if he had lost respect for me forever?

Survival Tip #17

How to Survive a Wildfire

- Obey all directives from emergency officials.

- Shut off the gas.

- Turn on all the lights inside and out so you are easier to spot.

- Move any furniture, curtains and other "kindling" away from windows and doors.

- Wet down the roof and shrubs.

- Fill sinks and bathtubs with cold water.

- Locate your evacuation kits.

    (Okay, we are not in that much danger here in Toronto. But all last year we had to watch British Columbia burn and people couldn't even breathe in Vancouver. And then there was Fort McMurray. Gas mask. I need gas masks.)

CHAPTER 17
I Want You to Panic

"Everyone is welcome to gather," we heard announced on a megaphone.

We all walked towards the picnic table under the big tree and gathered. There were about fifteen of us campers, and I noticed a lot of neighbours and their kids hanging around as well. There were a couple of reporters with big cameras. I also saw several cops standing off to the side. Many looked bored and hot, their arms crossed. An officer stood on the picnic table.

"Good evening. I'm Constable Davis," he said. "At this point, I want to make sure you understand we are not asking you to decamp. Protesters can continue with their protest. The city recognizes the rights of people to gather and participate in lawful and peaceful protest."

There were some cheers.

"We ask only that you cease burning fires. We also ask that you remove extension cords and equipment that has been unlawfully installed."

Groans. There goes our power.

He held up a paper. "This is a trespass order. If any of these terms are violated, you will be arrested."

"*That's a load of crap!*" screamed Kyle suddenly.

The officers on the edge of the crowd came to attention.

I saw Carol run up to Kyle, take him by the arm and try to calm him down. She led him away, murmuring quietly to him.

The officer stepped down and Jenny mounted the picnic table with her own megaphone. "Good afternoon, everyone," she called out. "I'm Jenny Laval. You all know why we're here!"

Cheers.

"We acknowledge the land we are meeting on," began Jenny, "as the traditional territory of many nations, including the Mississauga of the Credit, the Anishnabeg, the Chippewa, Haudenosaunee and the Wendat peoples, and is now home to many First Nations, Inuit and Métis peoples. We also acknowledge that Toronto is covered by Treaty 13 with the Mississaugas of the Credit. We at Climate Justice recognize that racialized people are more vulnerable to the effects of climate change."

A neighbour, who I recognized as one of the older dads on the street, called out, "I know it's happening. I just don't know what to do."

That surprised me. I realized I had felt like I was the only one in the world who cared. And now I was starting to see, as I looked around, that there were other people way more on top of this than I was.

"At least you are not doing climate change denial," responded Jenny. "We have to acknowledge Canada's massive footprint. We have to understand the money behind drilling for fossil fuels and the tar sands. We have to march on Ottawa next week and ask the government to get to net-zero emissions by 2030, to eliminate fossil fuel subsidies, and to stop the pipelines and cut greenhouse emissions. Let's take a look at meat, not just the terrible pain and inhumanity of factory farming, but its impact on the environment. Also, cutting meat and dairy can cut your carbon footprint by up to seventy-three per cent."

Well, that's it; I was never eating meat again.

"Our political system is designed to allow for protest. It is our right. It is our duty. Our leaders have not been listening to the scientists. Perhaps they will listen to our votes. I want to introduce you to one of our young leaders here in Canada, Ellen Benoit."

Wow! Ellen was here! She got up on the table. She was in a pink striped tank and jeans. Her face was sombre. I was impressed. She seemed really composed for her age.

"Hello, and thank you all for coming," she said in a clear, strong voice. "I know it takes a lot of courage to go up against big government and corporations. We want them to see what we see. We younger people are living in fear every day and watching the adults do *nothing*. We younger people are panicking about the environment. All we have heard all our lives is 'Reduce emissions . . . reduce emissions . . . you have twelve years . . . you have eight years.' Well, let me say something to our governmental officials."

She paused dramatically. She was very dramatic.

"You are going to die of old age and we are going to die of climate change!"

The crowd yelled its approval. I whooped aloud. Everyone here felt like me! I started to feel something in my stomach, something that wasn't a sinking pit. A calm glow. This was so much better than counting supplies alone in my room.

"Yes, we are panicked and I want you to panic," she continued. "I want you to feel the fear. And then I want you to *act*. I want you to act as you would in a crisis. I want you to act as if the house was on *fire*! Because it is."

"I'll tell you what, I'm impressed with these young people," a man behind me muttered to who I guessed was his wife. They were wearing matching Crocs. "What did we do about it?"

"Next week there will be a demonstration in Ottawa. I ask you all to join us in marching on the Capital."

More cheers.

Out of the corner of my eye I saw a food courier bike up. It was an Uber Eats delivery. Terence furtively jogged over to him and took the bag, then went back towards his tent. One of my sign-making buddies, Justine with the blue face, was waiting for him.

"Hello."

I jumped. It was Noor and George and Beth.

"I knew you were here," said Noor. She turned to George.

"George, go tell Mom and Dad we found her."

"Are there any hotdogs here?" asked George. It wasn't that weird a question. Every other time we'd been here, it was for a BBQ or community event.

"George!" hissed Noor.

"This is not fair!" he said and took off.

"You idiot," said Noor, turning to me.

I said nothing.

"A $2,000 generator? Really? You know that's fraud."

"I was going to pay for it."

"Jamilah, last I saw, you were looking for a solar flashlight on Bunz."

"Okay," I admitted. "I messed up. I can't do anything. I panicked."

"Just come home and fix it," she said. "I have seven hundred dollars in loonies from the coffee shop. I can help."

What? Seven hundred dollars?

"You have —" I started to say.

Suddenly we heard shouting over by the picnic table.

"This is bullcrap!"

Oh, no, it was Kyle again. He had jumped on the table with the megaphone.

"*Eff the police!*" he called out.

It looked like Kyle was having trouble regulating. The speeches and the cops must have stressed him out. The four or five cops who had been standing casually by the crowd straightened. They remained expressionless and seemed careful not to catch one another's eyes. Constable Davis ventured up to the table, his palms up and outstretched, trying not to look threatening, I guess.

"Kyle, get down," pleaded Jenny, reaching towards him.

Constable Davis continued to approach, and put one foot on the picnic bench. Kyle pulled the megaphone back and threw it into Constable Davis's face. Constable Davis half deflected it and fell. In an instant the bench was covered with officers dragging down and restraining Kyle. He screamed and twisted, kicking one female cop in the face. One of the officers pulled out a taser. I had never heard a sound before like the one Kyle made. It sounded like an elephant being strangled with a whine over it. Kyle went limp as the rest of the officers lined up in front of the crowd, who were circling the scene and capturing everything on their phones.

"Brutality!" people yelled as the police handcuffed Kyle on the ground.

I saw Jenny approach an officer and start talking quickly and earnestly. Then she was permitted to go to Kyle. Noor, Beth and I stood there the whole time with our hands over our mouths. Ellen Benoit was sobbing and being patted on the back by her mom.

Jenny spoke briefly to Constable Davis, then got up on the table. "Please peacefully disperse," she said. "We have legal counsel in hand for Kyle. He will be all right. Please obey the conditions the police laid out — no campfires and remove the extension cords from the field house."

Noor, Beth and I couldn't stop looking. But we had retreated to a large tree about twenty feet away from the scene. No one left.

About twenty minutes later, there were sirens, and paramedics rushed in with a stretcher. Kyle was gently transferred to the stretcher and, with Omar by his side, put into a waiting ambulance. Instead of leaving, people started gathering around even more. People were coming into the park. Kyle's arrest must have been posted on social media.

News crews started setting up and people started chanting. Some of them already had signs that said "Free Kyle" and "Defund the Police!"

"Free Kyle!"

"Free Kyle!"

"Jamilala, come home," said Noor. "You could get hurt here. Come home so Mom and Dad can kill you."

"You know what?" I said to Noor. "I can't. I'm going to see this through."

I couldn't go home yet. I had joined this group and I wasn't going to be like Terence the Tourist and go home to sleep when things got tough. Yes, I was shaken by Kyle. But this community had taken me in and I wasn't going to hide anymore. In that moment, I decided I was going to donate all my bunker food to the foodbank.

"No, you have been right," I continued. "I never do anything. It's all just for me. This time I'm going to do something with everyone."

"Okay," said Noor. "But we're staying, too."

"I gotta go pee," I said. "I'll meet you over there."

I pointed to where the news crew had set up. It seemed like the calmest area.

I walked over to the washroom in the field house. The stench was thick and three of the four toilets in the muddy stalls were clogged. There was no toilet paper. Thank God for my go bag. A city staffer was there, unplugging and rolling up an extension cord. I waited until he had left and peed. When I walked out, there was an officer outside the door. There were more park staff at my tent and Carol was taking down hers. It looked like we were being removed.

"Miss," said a man in a City of Toronto embossed shirt and cap. "You have to remove your tent and go."

"Okay, I'm leaving," I said.

"You got everything?" Carol asked me.

"Yup." I held up my go bag.

"I'll do your tent," she said. "It's okay."

"Thanks!"

I went over to where the crowd had gathered and was chanting, next to the news crew. Several officers with hands full of white zip ties stood side by side.

Seeing a news reporter in person was weird. They looked so small compared to how they appeared onscreen. This one was wearing false eyelashes and so much foundation it looked three dimensional. But her voice was steady and her back was straight. Jenny was beside her being interviewed. She gave me a thumbs-up.

"City staff are clearing a camp set up by climate change protesters in Dufferin Grove Park," the reporter said. "One protester was arrested after uttering threats and assaulting an officer."

The reporter gestured behind her.

"Scores of people are showing up to rally in the park in solidarity with the man who was arrested and charged," she said. "Here we have Jenny Laval, a leader in this climate change organization."

"This evening, what you see here, is the community coming out to support us," said Jenny. "At the same time, the city is evicting us, which is unfair. We've actually started to build long-lasting bonds with the community here."

The reporter looked back at the camera.

"The city is providing the protesters with time to gather their belongings, vacate their tents and temporarily vacate the protest area," she said. "City staff are removing unlawful items. In a statement, the city said it will store any of the items and equipment that the protesters have not taken with them and there will be a process for claiming them."

"Please vacate the perimeter. Please vacate the perimeter." It was an officer on a megaphone.

The police were now circling the crowd and sending them in a line down a path out of the park. I saw Officer Maclean, zip ties in his hand. A few protesters calmly sat on the ground. The police, four at a time, would lift them to their feet and zip-tie them, leading them to the curb to sit. I could see their guns. I could see their tasers.

The memory of Kyle being tasered was flashing in my mind.

"Free Kyle!"

"Free Kyle!"

"Free Kyle . . ."

The chanting was getting weaker. Jenny went to where people were getting arrested and quietly sat down.

I followed.

I had meant to get arrested bravely. But I couldn't help it — as soon as they pulled my arms back and put the zip ties on my wrists, I started crying. Let me tell you, it is such a drag to be crying when you can't wipe your face. They gently seated me next to Jenny on the curb.

"C'mon," said Jenny. "You can wipe your face on my shoulder."

When I lifted my snotty, tear-stained face, Officer Maclean was standing over me with a kind look. Around us were neighbours with their phones out.

"We got you, girl," one lady said. "It's okay, honey."

"Take it easy, kid," said Officer Maclean. "Don't worry. Nobody's going to hurt you."

I hiccupped. In my bleary vision I saw my dad approach from down the street, his sandals flapping. His plaid short-sleeved shirt was sweat-stained and he had an extremely worried look on his face. An officer held his arm out to stop him, so he halted, just within earshot.

"You kids are doing great things here, but you got to follow the law," said Officer Maclean.

"The officer is right," said Jenny. "Being arrested peacefully is a very powerful tool. It forces the legal system to examine our constitutional rights in action. It raises alarm bells for people who don't realize how dire human rights violations can be."

She looked me in the eye.

"It takes incredible courage and integrity," she said, "to do what you are doing. You should be proud."

Dad's face relaxed a bit and he nodded at me.

"Don't worry, *habibti*," he said. "I will be at the station for you."

Constable Davis came over and took Officer Maclean aside. They spoke quietly for a second and then Officer Maclean turned to me, leaned down and clipped off my ties.

"The city of Toronto has dropped all charges," he said. "You are free to go."

Survival Tip #18
How to Survive if You Get Caught in a Riptide

- Rip currents are channels of water that form near beaches on big bodies of water.
- If you get caught, don't fight the current.
- Swim parallel to the shore until you break out of the current.
- Then follow the waves at an angle back to land.

    (This will be helpful if I am stuck in a large crowd at the protest.)

CHAPTER 18
Road Trip

Dad made me do all the administration and organizing involved in returning the generator. It was a deeply frustrating experience — being put on hold, trying to find a way for it to be picked up (it was too heavy for our car) and having to suck up a restocking fee and the non-refundable delivery fee. It was hell. In the end, I owed Mom and Dad $375, which was okay. It would be my entire first paycheque with the solar company, but I was doing pretty good selling stuff from the garage.

I got the internship! Mrs. Vogel took me out on a few scouting missions to assess houses and roof pitches for solar panel installation and said I had a knack for engineering. I told her, yeah, but I had no math. She said she would tutor me, so I'm going to retake math at night school with her help. Apparently, it's incredibly common for girls to get left behind in math because of gender biases in teaching.

Then George declared he was going to be in IT, like Steve Jobs (who was Syrian!). But Noor told Dad not to worry, she was going to be a doctor. Like, at the very least.

It was the day before the March for Climate Change, and Vivian and I were in the driveway, packing Desmond's car for the trip. Mom and Dad were on the front porch watching. Of course, George was inside gaming till the last second.

Teta came out and gave us enough food for a week. Like all the church ladies, she put everything in aluminum. Fatayer, za'atar bread, boiled eggs (ick) and knafi. "I pray for you!" she called as we got in the car. She was babysitting Aziz and Leila later. The kids were almost finished fixing their bikes.

"George!" I shouted.

He came out, looking like he had just woken up, and got in the car.

"Wait," I said as we pulled out of the driveway. "I have to check the go bag one more time."

Desmond and George rolled their eyes at each other as I went to the trunk and pulled out my backpack.

"Aghh!" complained George.

"Hyper vigilance is important," scolded Vivian. "From a feminist perspective, women are neurologically designed to be more vigilant. You need to respect that."

"More vigilant and more mature," I said. "So there."

Water, check. Protein bars, check. Sewing kit, check. Duct tape — don't laugh, it can be used to fix cars or signs, and on warts — check. Swiss Army knife, check. N95 masks, check. Hydrogen peroxide in case of tear gas, check. Flashlight, check. Band-Aids, check. Pain reliever, extra socks, check and check.

"Jam, come on!" complained Desmond.

"Okay, just one second," I said. I had to check my fanny pack. Mini versions of everything, including a compass and matches and a magnifying glass. Guiltily, I touched the vape pen I had put in an inner pocket. I had almost thrown it out last night. I was only doing two hits a day and the cartridge was basically empty. But, I thought, if I was about to get arrested tomorrow, it might help me not cry.

We ate some of the snacks in the first two hours of the four-hour trip to Ottawa, listening to Desmond's brilliant playlist —

a mix of top hits, his parents' old favourites and a few Palestinian pop artists for George and me. About halfway along the highway, we went by a beautiful lake you could drive up to with picnic tables. So we pulled over and got out. It was about noon and there was a slight breeze. The sun glinted off the ripples on the water and a tree whispered above us. About forty feet away was a sandy beach.

"Let's swim," said George, as we were opening the food containers.

"Yeah!" said Desmond.

We changed into our gear, which for George and Desmond meant taking off their T-shirts and putting on swim trunks. Viv and I just put tank tops on over our bike shorts. We ran to the water and stopped. The water was thick with a brilliant green coating.

"Wait." Vivian pointed to a sign.

"BEACH TEMPORARILY CLOSED DUE TO BLUE-GREEN ALGAE"

"Oh, yeah," I said. "I read about this. Too much sewage and farm runoff gets into the lake."

"Man!" said George.

"Well," said Desmond. "Add it to the sign slogans."

We went back to the picnic table. I started putting all the food back in the containers.

"You know what?" I said. "I don't even want to be near this. Let's just eat in the car."

We piled back in and drove on. We were quiet for about twenty minutes until Desmond said, "Onwards, my warriors, to the next battle!" in a dumb video-game-soldier voice. He put on the music. We laughed and hooted, fists in the air. Soon we were singing along and passing around the snacks.

The first thing we did when we got to Aunt Janice and Uncle Phil's bungalow on a tree-lined street was storm the pool.

Aunt Janice and Uncle Phil brought out lemonade and sandwiches and watched, their French bulldog circling the water's edge and barking hysterically.

"But pools, you know —" I started to say.

"Jammy Jam," said Vivian, grabbing my arm. "Give it a rest for today. We can't solve everything all at once and we have to refuel to fight another day!"

"*Cannonball!*" screamed George and whipped past me. I squealed when the water splashed on me. Then I laughed. Okay, but we were making a sign against water crises as well.

Aunt Janice ordered us pizza and put us all in the basement rec room. The girls got the fold-out couch and the boys got air mattresses on the floor. We watched an old movie and everyone else slowly dozed off before me.

I turned off the TV and started mind looping about the march. The old anxiety came back as I pictured the crowds and police. But I looked over at Desmond on the floor, so cutely asleep, and felt better. Besides, even Aunt Janice, in her orthotic shoes, was going to march.

How bad could it get?

Survival Tip #19

Duck and Cover

Duck and cover was a 1950s campaign to teach kids how to protect themselves in case of a nuclear bomb.

When a siren went off, kids had to crawl under their desks to hide, like a turtle in its shell.

(This is how you know you can't totally trust governments and you better take care of yourself.)

CHAPTER 19
The March

Noor and Beth had gone to Ottawa on the LGBTQ2 bus. Noor texted that she would meet up with us in Confederation Park, which is a pretty park with a huge fountain near Parliament Hill. Uncle Phil dropped us off a few blocks away because the streets were full of protesters. We walked to the fountain and I looked around, shouldering my heavy bag. The streets around the park were lined with old-fashioned heritage buildings, side by side with big, ugly government towers.

It was a beautiful September day with a nice breeze. People were streaming in from all sides and I was surprised at how gentle the vibe was. It had more of a music festival atmosphere than a protest. There was even a man playing guitar and singing. And there were so many kids, it looked like a birthday party. I guess it made sense that kids were there. It was their future. A lot of the kids had face paint on like it was a birthday party, too. The kids' signs included:

"MY CHILDREN WILL BE AN ENDANGERED SPECIES"

"WHY SHOULD I CLEAN MY ROOM WHEN THE WORLD IS A MESS?"

I even saw a toddler in a stroller clutching a sign that said:

"DON'T BURN MY FUTURE."

I took a picture of that one to send to Mom and Dad for the next time they thought I was overreacting. There was quite a police presence around, officers in their bulletproof vests and no expression on their faces. But after my encounter in Dufferin Grove, I wasn't that scared of them. Besides, I knew now what to do if I got arrested.

A dad talking to a news reporter tried to get his little girl to hold her sign right side up. The little girl frowned and clenched the handle closer to her body, resting the poster on the ground. Desmond and I looked at each other and laughed.

"Cool, eh?" he said.

I kissed him lightly. This wasn't making me nervous at all. With all the kids around it was almost boring.

"Aunt Janice!" Noor and Beth came running up.

Aunt Janice looked at Noor's lavender crew cut. "Wow," she said, hugging Noor.

A chant started.

"Climate change? *Non, merci*!"

"Well," said Aunt Janice, "let's go." She held up her sign. It was handwritten and had "This is for older women who cannot attend" written in Magic Marker. It had signatures from her older friends in the neighbourhood.

We started to move towards the looming castle up the street. Parliament Hill is an incredibly bizarre and beautiful place. It's like five castles from old England got dumped on a cliff next to a wild Canadian river. And then there's the Rideau Canal beside it, which looks like a medieval moat. When we got to the huge front lawn, there were people lying on blankets like it was a picnic. All over were clusters of protesters holding signs representing Indigenous peoples, Black Lives Matter, BIPOC and LGBTQ activist groups.

"Look," said Vivian. She pointed to a girl who looked to be about eleven years old in a hijab, with a handwritten sign on her chest that said "THIS PLANET NEEDS YOU TO GIVE A SHIT."

For people coming together to fight the end of the world, it was a very smiley crowd. It had a very different feel from the encampment. It was like, because everyone was there to support each other, everyone felt safe. Except for the chanting, people generally talked quietly and strangers smiled at each other.

"Hey hey! Ho ho! Fossil fuels have got to go!"

Vivian went ahead to get a good spot by the stage so Desmond and I went to hang with the Black Lives Matter group. I do have to admit, the Black protesters were a bit more guarded, but still proud, dedicated and joyful. We hung out with them for a while until I started to get very tired and hot. The sun blazed on the parched lawn and there was no shade anywhere.

"What do we want?"

"Climate Justice!"

"When do we want it?"

"Now!"

Wait! The person on the megaphone was Jenny! In one hand she was holding the megaphone and with the other she was struggling with one end of a seven-foot-long banner that read simply "CLIMATE JUSTICE." Carol was holding up the other end. I waved and jumped up and down.

"Jamilah!" called Jenny. "Come grab this side of the banner."

I ran up and grabbed it from her, giving her a quick side hug. Then I stood there holding up the banner. I never thought I would be so relaxed in such a big crowd. But I was starting to feel a bit sick from the sun. The breeze had gone and it was 2 p.m.

"What do we want?"

"Climate Justice!"

"When do we want it?"

"Now!"

Toddlers were starting to whine a bit, too. It really was very

145

hot. Ahead of me, a teen girl suddenly dropped to sit cross-legged, and her mother leaned over her, concerned. I felt a bit dizzy. Heatstroke or sunstroke? I ran through my mental survival checklist. I had to hydrate and cover my head. I handed the end of the sign to Desmond.

"You okay?" he asked.

"Yeah," I said. "I just need to take a minute."

Well, there was nowhere for me to go. And I sure wasn't going to be famous for being the person who died of sunstroke at a climate change march. I had to bloom where I was planted. I carefully sat down and opened my go bag, pulling out my kaffiyeh, water and the first aid kit. Taking the water, I sipped a little and drenched my hair then put my cotton sunhat on. Better.

"Could you move back a bit?" I asked the people around me.

"Sure. You okay?" they asked. It wasn't that big a crowd. There were thousands of people, not hundreds of thousands. They moved back. I made some shade by jamming my protest sign into the ground and draping the kaffiyeh over it. Better. I pulled out my battery-operated fan. In two minutes, I was comfortable. A whining toddler was close to me in a stroller, so we were on the same level. I smiled up at the mom. "Okay?" I asked holding up the fan.

"Sure," she said.

It was so cute. As soon as the little breeze hit his face, the kid blinked and tried to grab at the fan. His mom put a little water on his face and he started to doze off. There. We had cooled him down.

People came up to speak, including our prime minister, whose speech, considering his support of big companies, was surprisingly radical. It was great, but I would be very surprised if he did all the things he said he was going to do. A musician came on next.

Aunt Janice plopped down beside me. "Whew," she said. "Do you have any sunscreen in that supply cupboard of yours?"

"For face or body?" I asked.

"You know," said Aunt Janice, "when I was in school, we used to have drills to learn how to protect ourselves from nuclear bombs."

"What?" I asked. "Whole bombs?"

We had had drills for school shootings, which were pretty scary in themselves, with all the students curled up against one wall of the classroom. But not for nuclear bombs.

"Yeah, there was an arms race around the world and everyone was afraid of a nuclear bomb," said Aunt Janice. "They actually thought you could protect yourself from radiation by hiding under your desk. They called it Duck and Cover."

"How did you not go crazy?" I asked.

"Who says we didn't?" grinned Janice. "Just after that came the wild sixties, and everyone partied for, like, a decade. Jamilah," she said seriously. "It's important to enjoy life as well as be a responsible citizen, you know."

"I like the clothes from then," I said.

"I might have some old pieces for you," said Aunt Janice. "I was a bit bigger than you when I was your age."

Hmm, it would be nice not to wear bike shorts and a T-shirt all the time.

The protest was starting to thin out. Vivian ran up.

"That was awesome!" she said. "C'mon, let's go."

* * *

It was such a relief to be back in Aunt Janice and Uncle Phil's cool basement rec room. We were exhausted and, after jumping in the pool and eating hotdogs (Aunt Janice had wisely bought veggie ones, too), only wanted to be in the dim cave. Maybe that's what all humans really want, a cave. Desmond and George had managed to find an ancient video game system of Uncle Phil's. Viv and I lounged on the air mattresses, sorting through the brightly coloured mini-dresses Aunt Janice had dug up.

"You see," said Vivian. "It wasn't so bad. Maybe next time, we can drive down to Washington."

"Uh, no," I said. "I draw the line at an armed protest. But there's plenty to do right here. We have the wind farms and solar power. And the corporations really have to give more of their taxes . . ."

"Okay, okay! Slow down," laughed Vivian.

"And I think I'm going to become vegetarian," I said. "It's gonna kill Teta. But we have to protest factory farming — it's got to stop. You know, I bet I could build a chicken coop in the backyard and rescue some chickens."

"Oh, God, I hope this solar job keeps you too busy for that," said Vivian. "Come on, let's try on these dresses!"

She turned the music up on her phone and we slipped into the brightly coloured shifts, dancing and laughing. They hadn't invented size zero in the sixties, so the dresses were super comfortable. Aunt Janice was right, it was okay, even necessary, to have a little fun sometimes. I let the familiar low buzz of worry lift a little from my chest. It was a good day's work. Joining with organizations and other people felt so much more powerful than trying to do it on my own.

I was still going to get that generator for the bunker, though. And Teta was going to love those chickens.

ACKNOWLEDGEMENTS

I'd like to acknowledge the young people who are protesting and educating us, whether it be about climate or land rights. My newcomer father Louis Francis Zeitoun and his brothers Uncle Anis, Uncle Ralph, Uncle Gaby, Uncle Tony and Uncle Ralph, who had the courage to leave and Aunt Alice and her family, who had the courage to stay. The support of my siblings Francis, Paul and Randa, who also provided exacting research and text pep talks, my friends and editors including Kat Mototsune, Mary Dickie, Melanie Little and Sharon English, the Arts Councils of Canada, Ontario and Toronto, especially their Deaf and Disability Arts Programs. Thanks to Lee Maracle for her generous insight, Angelo Colussi and other allies, my writing godfathers Maurice Grimes, John Metcalf, Michael Helm and Roddy Doyle. Special thanks to the Toronto Palestinian Film Festival, which has provided me and my extended family validation, joy and visibility. The "Diverse" Canadian and Turtle Island writers group and the comic stylings of DJ Khaled, the Hadids, the El Salomons, Maysoon Zayid and Amer Zahr. We are here. We are here. So there.